The Mathematical Princess

Other children's books by Robert Nye

March Has Horse's Ears
Taliesin
Beowulf: A New Telling
Wishing Gold

The Mathematical Princess

and Other Stories

Robert Nye

Illustrated by
Paul Bruner

Hill & Wang · New York
A division of Farrar, Straus and Giroux

Illustrations copyright © 1972 by Hill & Wang,
a division of Farrar, Straus & Giroux, Inc.,
except illustrations on pages 33, 36, and 47,
© 1971 by Macmillan & Co., Ltd

Text copyright © 1971 by Robert Nye

First American printing, 1972
ISBN: 0-8090-6806-0
Library of Congress catalog card number: 79-185428
Published simultaneously in Canada by Doubleday Canada Ltd, Toronto
Printed in the United States of America

Originally published in Great Britain as *Poor Pumpkin*

1 2 3 4 5 6 7 8 9 10

For my daughter Rebecca

Contents

The

Mathematical

Princess

Old King Cole of Colchester had one daughter,
and she was the most beautiful girl in all the land.
Her name was Clare. She had black hair and
green eyes, and she was very good at mathematics.
Unfortunately, being so clever with numbers
made Clare scorn the more ordinary things in life.
She never went out to run barefoot in dewy grass,
or sip the cream off the milk, or sniff the scent of
roses after rain. Her days were stern and lonely.
She spent them mostly in her private schoolroom,
busy with chalk at a little blackboard. Teachers
came from all over Britain, giving her lessons in
square roots, conic sections and vulgar fractions.

By the time Clare grew up she knew more than all the teachers added together and multiplied by six. She used to set herself Examinations. She had no brothers and sisters so she always came top, simply because there was nowhere else to come. She would have been top anyway, because she never once got an answer wrong.

One day, her father, old King Cole, decided that the time had come for Clare to marry. Because she was so clever he saw he had a problem. He did not want her husband to be unworthy of her. It would have to be a brainy man. So he called Clare to him and said:

"Daughter, here is my plan. Every suitor that comes to court asking for your hand will be set this test. He is to sit up all night with you in the schoolroom. While he sits there you will talk about the principles of the mathematician Euclid. Talk in the cleverest way you can."

"But, Father," said Clare, "what if the man does not understand? He will be bored."

"Exactly," said the King. "And if he is bored, he will fall asleep. And every one that falls asleep will lose his head in the morning! If we do it this way we can be sure of getting the right husband for you, my dear, and not have our time wasted by fools and fortune-seekers."

Clare thought privately that her father's plan was more than a little cruel. But she did what he said.

Now King Cole was a very rich and powerful man. All this was in the long-ago time when Britain was divided into many little kingdoms, and the kingdom of Colchester was one of the most important. So when the news spread that the Princess was for marrying, lords came from all over the country to try to win her hand. Some went home again when they learned that they would have their heads cut off if they failed to stay awake all night while Clare talked about Euclid. But those who considered themselves intelligent would rather have died than fail to submit to the test.

The first night there were two suitors in the schoolroom. Clare began to talk. She was shy and uncertain at first. But she was so passionately interested in what she was talking about that it was not long before she forgot her audience completely and rattled on in full spate. The two men concentrated hard. But crafty old King Cole had taken care to give them a heavy meal and several bottles of wine before beginning. Before long their attention began to wander. They yawned. Their eyes went up and down the room, seeking for something to hold their interest awake. Meanwhile, hardly pausing to catch her breath, Clare went on and on:

". . . the base angles of an isoceles triangle are equal . . . this is elementary, axiomatic . . . as Aristotle said, 'You must begin somewhere, and you start with things admitted but undemonstrable' . . . so the line *CD* divides the triangle *ABC* into two triangles *ACD* and *CDB*, and *AC* equals *CB*, because the original triangle . . . regular polyhedra . . . doubling the cube, of course . . . and so the point *P* where the line *AP* and the angle *PB* . . . whereas ellipses and circles and hyperbolas and parabolas . . ."

That was how it sounded to the two poor suitors. Try as they might, they could not keep pace with the princess's argument, and it all came through to them in little bits and pieces, dry and boring and terribly difficult to follow.

They fidgeted. They tried ignoring her and adding up in their heads just how much money they would get in her dowry. But she was so beautiful their eyes kept coming back to her face. And looking at her face made them feel sleepy, because her voice went on and on and on and on.

"The seventy-first theorem states . . ."

One of them tried to stop the flood of words by asking her questions. But his questions were stupid and, besides, Clare was too engrossed in Euclid to pay any heed to him.

"The seventy-second theorem is even more interesting, because . . ."

The first one fell asleep at theorem eighty-two. The other, by biting his tongue and pulling his fingers until they cracked, managed to stay awake until theorem ninety-nine. Theorem one hundred was told to a room full of snores.

"It's rather a pity," Clare said to her father, after the royal executioner had taken them off.

"Fiddlesticks," snapped King Cole. "They asked for it. Silly beggars. Probably only interested in your money. Deserve all they get. Beheading's too good for them, really."

"Oh," breathed Clare, shaking her long black tresses. "I wasn't thinking of the beheading bit."

"What's rather a pity, then?" demanded her father.

"That one of them missed four hundred and eighteen theorems and the other four hundred and one," said Clare. "There are five hundred altogether, you know, in Euclid's *Elements*."

"Of course I know," the King said hurriedly, because he didn't know at all. He went off humming and rubbing his hands, looking forward to the pipe and bowl that comprised his usual breakfast. Then a sudden thought struck him and he came back.

"Do you mean you went on talking about the whole five hundred?" he said. "Even after they fell asleep?"

"Oh yes," said Clare.

"But my dear girl," said the King, "there was no need for that."

"Then you should have said so," Clare pointed out. "I'm a very methodical person, you know."

"I thought I did know," said King Cole. "But I know even better now."

"Anyway," said Clare in a grand voice, "Mathematics does not cease just because two ignorant fellows fall asleep. It goes on. And on. It could go on for ever, you know."

Her father backed away as though she had threatened him. "I know, I know," he muttered quickly. "I know, I know."

And he trotted off down the corridor, shivering at the squeak of Clare's chalk on the blackboard behind him.

Several more suitors came. They suffered the same fate as the first two. Clare said she was very upset to have these men falling asleep as she was talking to them. It was rude and she did not like it. King Cole chuckled nervously. She told him to put a sign over the door of the schoolroom, warning fools to keep away. So he did. It was the same sign that had hung hundreds of years before at the entrance to the philosopher Plato's Academy. It said:

LET NO ONE IGNORANT
OF MATHEMATICS
ENTER HERE

At last, suitors stopped coming altogether. Clare sat at her blackboard doing complicated calculations to work out her exact chance of getting a husband. She knew the answer before she started. It was 0.

She grew miserable. Numbers did not seem enough any more. Sometimes she looked out from the tall turret window and saw the grass below blowing in the wind. A field full of it was like a land-locked sea, great shifting waves of green flowing with light and air. Clare had never seen the sea, so she was not able to make this comparison. Her gaze perceived only angles and patterns of light. But these did not explain the tears which came to her eyes in her long looking.

She tried constructing a planetarium to pass the time. It was very good but she soon grew bored with it. She invented a system of levers and pulleys to bring the food up from the royal kitchens to the royal dining-hall and designed a glass that would ease the King's sciatica by focusing the sun's rays on a small point in the middle of his back. She read a lot — Cosmas's *Topographia Christiana*, which had just come out, was her favourite, closely followed by Archimedes' *The Sand Reckoner*. These helped, but sometimes Clare could not concentrate on the pages because of the tears that kept gathering in her green eyes. She wept for all the men who had been killed because they fell asleep. She wept for herself because no one was clever enough to marry her.

Under a bridge about a mile from Colchester Castle, a young man sat washing his feet. His name was Walt, and he was a shepherd. He had hair like a bird's nest and a good smile. He wore a red shirt and white breeches. He had no shoes.

Walt's feet were sore because he had walked a long way. He leaned back against the mossy bank and wriggled his toes where they were plunged in the cool running water. It was delicious to feel it flowing against his skin. He was a lively, down-to-earth person, not too bright in the head but quick to enjoy things that could be felt, or smelt, or tasted. His only possessions were a shepherd's white crook and a bottle and a bag. They lay on the grass beside him now.

An old friar in a patched hood, crossing the bridge, looked down at the lad sprawled idle in the sun, and snorted.

"No work to do, and a strong fellow like you?" he called in a sour voice.

Walt gazed up lazily, shielding his eyes with his hand. "I'm a shepherd, father."

"Then where are your sheep, my son?"

Walt shrugged. "I left them with my master, many miles away. I'm journeying to Colchester to marry the Princess Clare."

The friar burst out laughing. Then he put on a serious face and stabbed the air with his forefinger as he spoke. "Turn round now," he said, "and go back home to your sheep where you belong. Haven't you heard that the Princess will only marry a man as clever as herself? What chance have you, a stupid shepherd, where some of the wisest princes in Christendom have failed?"

Walt did not answer. A trout was nibbling at his toes in the light-speckled water. Quickly he bent and snatched it from the river. He held it up, wriggling, in the sun. Then he tossed it from hand to hand, delighted at the catch.

"Do you hear me, my son?" the friar demanded.

"Yes," said Walt. "I hear you."

"And do you know the penalty if you fail, as you certainly will fail?" pursued the friar.

"Yes," said Walt. "I know the penalty."

He popped the fish into his bag and resumed his sprawl, hands tucked behind his head.

The friar's beads flashed in a loop of light. "You go to your death," he warned.

Walt grinned. "Either a king's daughter or a headless shepherd," he called gaily. "All my life they've told me my head is my weakest part. I reckon I can get along without it just as well."

Another trout was nibbling at his toes. He snatched it out of the water as deftly as he had caught the first. The fish made his bag thump when he dropped it in.

"That's a useful trick," said the friar.

"No trick really," said Walt. "I'm good at these things."

"Then why not sit there all day?" the friar suggested, losing patience with him. "At least you wouldn't come to any harm. You've got ideas above your station, that's your trouble."

When the friar had gone, Walt sat wondering if there was any truth in what the man had said. He was only a shepherd, and he respected people like the friar — wise men, who seemed to know so much more about the ways of the world. But when he thought of going home his eyes pricked with tears. He had to go on. He had to see the Princess. He had dreamed about her and in his dream he had known she was beautiful. He felt sure he was going to fall in love with her at first sight. And Walt was a person who trusted his feelings. His head might not be much good, but his heart was usually right.

Another trout came nibbling his toes, and another, and another. Walt's capable hands moved swiftly through the water. He put them in his bag with the others. Then he filled his bottle with fresh stream water, took up his shepherd's white crook, and went on his way to Colchester.

Old King Cole laughed when he saw Walt. And old King Cole's chamberlain laughed. And old King Cole's barber, and old King Cole's cook, and old King Cole's thirteen page boys — they all laughed when they saw him. But Clare did not laugh.

"What do you want?" demanded the King, who was smoking one of his favourite pipes, made of bronze. (Tobacco, of course, had not yet been introduced to Europe, and he smoked a foul-smelling mixture of aromatic herbs that made the courtiers wince every time he puffed out.)

Walt said politely, "I want to marry your daughter, if it pleases you, your majesty."

"It certainly doesn't," said the King.

"Oh," said Walt.

"Well?" said the King.

"Nothing," said Walt. "Just oh, really."

King Cole wiped his fingers on his black beard and drank a bowl of mead in one go. He was not usually such a hearty man, but he could not help showing off in front of strangers. Particularly when they were strangers who looked as though they could easily be impressed — like Walt.

"I heard there was a test," Walt said. "And that there was no rule forbidding shepherds to try. To win your daughter's hand, I mean."

"You're after her money of course," the King snapped.

Walt blinked. "No, I'm not!" he said. "I love her."

"Love?" laughed King Cole. "Love doesn't come into this. It's a question of mathematics." He beckoned his daughter to him. "Did you hear what this ignorant lout just said?" he demanded.

"I heard," said Clare. There were tears in her eyes. "It's too much," she went on, her normally precise voice choking to keep back sobs. "I shall be the laughing-stock of Britain at this rate. Nobody wants to marry me. Nobody is fit to be my husband. The wisest princes have all failed and now your enemies send a silly shepherd with no shoes to mock me!"

King Cole glared across at Walt, who was shifting his bag from hand to hand. "You," he said. "You with the shepherd's crook! Go away before I have your head off!"

Walt took a deep breath. "I'm quite ready to lose my head," he said. "But at least let me lose it in trying the test."

Clare stared hard at him. She saw the scribbles of mud on his white breeches and the holes in his red shirt. Weeping, she ran from the room.

King Cole gnawed at his beard. He was now very angry indeed. At last, after a terrible silence, he spoke to Walt. His voice was dangerously quiet. "Very well," he said. "Go to the kitchens and they will give you some scraps to eat. Present yourself at the royal schoolroom on the last stroke of ten. You shall have your chance, since you insist on it. But at dawn tomorrow you will discover the reward for such impudence."

Then he called the royal executioner to him and told him not to use the best axe.

The clock struck ten. Walt was already waiting in the schoolroom. He had washed his feet and combed his hair. His shepherd's white crook lay propped against the blackboard. He had his bag in one hand and his bottle in the other.

Clare swept in without so much as a glance at him. She went straight to the blackboard and began talking.

". . . In the circle ACH, let AOH be a diameter, and let CE be the sine of the arc CH, or of the angle COH, and of its supplement COA. The sine of a quadrant . . ."

"A what?" said Walt.

Clare spun round. Her green eyes were blazing. "Don't interrupt me, peasant!" she hissed.

"Sorry," Walt said good-temperedly. "But what is a sine?"

"I thought everybody knew that," said Clare.

"Well, I don't," said Walt, and grinned.

Despite herself, Clare grinned back at him. Her anger suddenly melted away. Was it because Walt had such a handsome smile, she wondered. Or was it because none of the previous suitors, nor her father, nor even her teachers for that matter, had ever dared admit that they did not know something? Both probably, thought Clare. The young man's smile *was* good to see, and it was certainly refreshing to hear someone actually saying they did not understand her, instead of pretending they did and eventually falling asleep out of sheer boredom.

"A sine," she explained, "is a line drawn from one end of an arc, perpendicular to the radius drawn through the other end, and always equal to half the chord of double the arc." She drew a diagram on the blackboard. The chalk squealed. "You see?"

Walt scratched his head. "No," he admitted frankly.

Clare found some of her original annoyance coming back. The young man was an idiot. "A quadrant," she went on, determined to drive him to sleep like the others, "is the quarter of a circle, or of the circumference of a circle. Thus, the sine of a quadrant is equal to the radius, and the sine of any arc is half the chord of twice the arc, and . . ."

"What lovely eyes you have," said Walt.

Clare blushed. Her fingers flew to her cheeks. "About conic sections," she stammered. "When the cutting plane passes through the apex . . ."

"And your hair is like a raven's wing," said Walt. "I've seen sloe berries like that, but not so black."

"Slow berries?" said Clare, fascinated by the idea. "How can a berry be slow?"

"I don't know," admitted Walt, "but everyone calls them that."

Clare sniffed. "It seems to me," she said haughtily, "that there's rather a lot you don't know."

"That's right," said Walt. "Tell you one thing I do know, though."

"What's that?"

Walt smiled again. "Shut your eyes and cross your fingers and I'll tell you," he promised. "It's for luck."

"Luck?" scoffed Clare. "I've heard about *that*. The Law of Probability is one thing — but superstition is for stupid people." Nevertheless, she shut her eyes and crossed her fingers, curious to hear what he had to say.

"I love you," said Walt.

"How unmathematical," Clare protested, opening her eyes and turning back to the blackboard. "Now, the first theorem of Euclid states . . ."

"Will you marry me?" said Walt.

"The man who marries me," said Clare coolly, "has to keep awake all night while I talk about mathematics. You know that."

Walt grinned again. "Arithmetic is not the only thing that counts," he said.

Clare clapped her hands. She thought this a wonderfully witty remark. She had felt confused because her feelings about this shepherd were so up and down — liking him one moment, hating him the next. She was not very good at feelings, she realised. But she imagined that he was. At once she began to hope secretly that he would win — that he would pass her father's absurd test, keep awake all night, and win her hand. But she did not dare help him. That would not be fair.

"You," she said, pretending anger, "you're just a vulgar fraction!"

And she pressed on with the first hundred theorems.

Walt did not understand a word of what she was saying. Her voice sounded pleasant to him, reminding him of cool green grass and the chat of streams over shelves of white pebbles. As the clock struck midnight he began to nod with sleep.

Clare glanced at him in dismay. "Oh, dear shepherd," she whispered softly, "I've caught you napping!"

The tenderness in her tone made Walt snap awake. Quickly he bent and plunged his hand in his bag. "Oh no, dear princess," he said, "I was busy fishing."

"Fishing?" said Clare. "There's no fish-pond in this schoolroom!"

"No matter for that," said Walt. "Look!"

And, grinning broadly, he held up one of the trout he had caught that day.

Again Clare clapped her hands for joy. "It's lovely!" she cried. "So silver and clean." She touched it gently with her fingers all powdered with dry chalk. "Can you catch one for me?" she asked shyly.

"Maybe I can," said Walt, "when I have baited my hook." And he touched his fingers to hers and then dipped his hand into the bag again, bringing out the second trout, which was smaller than the first, but even prettier.

Clare held the little fish cradled in her hands. She stared at it for a long time. When she looked up at Walt he saw that her green eyes were full of tears. "Dear shepherd," she said, "I think you are good at the things I am bad at." Walt nodded slowly. Then he drew out a third fish and laid it on her copy of *Euclid*.

In the morning old King Cole came to the schoolroom in a great hurry, the royal executioner at his heels, but when Clare saw the axe she cried out, "There's no work for you today."

"What?" said her father. "Hasn't the shepherd slept?"

"Not a wink," said Clare.

The King grew angry, suspecting a trick. "Then you didn't talk mathematics all night!" he shouted. "You've deceived me, you wicked, wicked girl! Off with his head! Off, off with —"

"Father," said Clare, who was standing hand in hand with Walt, "all this ranting and raving doesn't suit you one little bit. You're not very good at it, you know." She bit her tongue and grinned at Walt. "Oops, sorry," she said.

"You say sorry to a shepherd?" stuttered the King.

"Yes," said Clare. "He noticed that I keep saying 'you know' at the end of every sentence, as though *I* know everything and expect everyone else to know it too. It's a shocking bad habit."

King Cole swallowed hard. "Did you or did you not put him to the proper test?" he demanded. "Because if you didn't talk mathematics all night, then —"

"Oh," said Clare, "I talked half the night and Walt talked the other. Quite a good arrangement. He knows about all sorts of things I don't. And when he wasn't talking, he was fishing."

"Now I know you're lying," said the King. "Fishing! In the schoolroom? Impossible!"

"That's right," said Clare. "Walt is very good at the impossible." And she showed her father the three trout.

Now old King Cole began to laugh. Clare was talking to him in a new voice — kinder, gentler, much easier to listen to. He realised that he had always been a bit afraid of his clever daughter. If this shepherd had helped her to be more human, then why not let them marry? He wasn't a snob, after all. Not a bit of it. Indeed, he was a merry old soul at heart, given half a chance for merriment. And shepherds *did* marry princesses, sometimes, in stories; he'd heard about it. "I say, son-in-law," he said shyly, "can you catch me a fish too?"

Walt put his hand into the bag for the last time and drew out the biggest trout of all. King Cole was very pleased.

"Ho!" he cried. "I'll have it stuffed in honour of the occasion. Bring me my pipe! Bring me my bowl! And where are those three wretched violinists of mine?"

So Walt the shepherd and the Princess Clare were married, and there was dancing and singing and merrymaking in the kingdom of Colchester for a whole week. And they lived very happily, making a fine couple, Clare with her head, Walt with his heart, and each of them learning from the other, ever after.

Poor Pumpkin

There was once a farmer called Farmer who had three sons. Their names were Peter, Paul, and Pumpkin. Peter was strong and Paul was clever but poor little Pumpkin was no use for anything. He could not run and he could not do sums. His father was always hitting him on the head and telling him to grow up. Pumpkin did not complain but he was not happy. It was not just his father hitting him on the head that made him sad. In fact in a way he did not mind the hitting very much, because it made him know what he was sad about. When there was no hitting and he still felt sad Pumpkin felt it was worst of all. Then the tears ran down his face like raindrops.

One day Peter came to his father and said:

"Father, I'm off into the world to make my fortune."

"That's my boy," said his father approvingly, and gave him a walking stick to help him on his way.

Peter took the walking stick and set out for London. He had not gone far when he met an old lady riding a green bicycle with white wheels and the spokes of the wheels all the colours of the rainbow. "Good morning, Peter," she said, dismounting. "Where are you off to?"

Peter was surprised that the old lady knew his name. She was wearing spectacles. One side it was blue glass and the other red. Peter did not much like the look of her. "I'm off into the world to make my fortune," he said briskly, and tried to push past her.

"Wait a linnet," cried the old lady. "There's no need to go any further. You can make your fortune right here and now."

"Here?" said Peter laughing. And he looked up and down for the road was lonely.

"And now," said the old lady, not laughing at all and grabbing hold of the end of his walking stick. "Tell me true, what to do for you: ten thousand pounds, your own hotel business, or to learn my art?"

Peter thought the question was ridiculous. The old girl must be mad, he said to himself. But he was a young man who knew what he wanted, so he said aloud: "Give me the ten thousand pounds, anyday!"

"Anyday, someday, never, *now!*" cackled the old lady, fumbling in the saddlebag of her bicycle. She took out ten thousand pounds in used one-hundred-pound notes and handed him the bundle. Then she stood on one pedal of her bicycle, gave it a push with her other foot, threw her leg over the saddle, and made off, pedalling merrily, not looking back.

Peter stared at the money as if he suspected that it would crumble to dust in his hands. Then he gave a whoop of delight, threw his walking stick over the sun, and went home. When he told his father about his good luck, and showed him the ten thousand pounds, his father loved him all the more for it.

About a year later, Paul, the middle son, the one who was clever, came to the father and said:

"Father, I'm off into the world to make my fortune."

"Good lad," said his dad. He looked out of the window and saw that there were some big black clouds about, so he gave Paul an umbrella to keep the rain off his head with all the brains in it.

Paul put up the umbrella and set out for London. Just past Woking it stopped raining and he saw a rainbow right down the road and through the middle of the rainbow came an old lady riding on a green bicycle with white wheels and the spokes of the wheels one red, one orange, one yellow, one green, one blue, one indigo, one violet, in that order, going round and round twinkling in the sun and lovely to see. "Good morning, Paul," she called, dismounting. "Where are you off to?"

Paul was startled that this old lady seemed to know who he was. She was wearing spectacles. One side it was yellow glass and the other side violet. Paul did not like the look of her at all. "I'm off into the world to make my fortune," he said quickly. "Move your bike, missus, you're in my way!"

"Hold your larks," said the old lady. "There's no need to go wearing your feet out. You can make your fortune right this minute where you're standing."

Paul jumped in the air and looked under his shoes. But he was only pretending. He did not really believe the old lady. He thought she was crazy. Laughing, he poked at her with his umbrella.

The old lady caught hold of the end of it. "Tell me true," she cackled, "what to do for you: ten thousand pounds, your own hotel business, or to learn my art?"

Now Paul was clever. He didn't want ten thousand pounds when he knew that to have your own hotel business might bring in that amount every year for the rest of your life. So although he didn't think the old lady had any power to give him what he wanted, he said aloud: "The hotel business for me, thanks!"

"Thanks, cranks, pink tanks, *banks!*" chanted the old lady. She fished in the saddlebag of her bicycle and handed Paul a piece of paper, neatly folded. When Paul had unfolded it, this is what he read:

TO WHOM IT MAY CONCERN: this is to certify that Paul Farmer Esq. is the sole & rightful owner proprietor master & overmaster of the following hotels, viz., the Ritz, the Carlton, the Savoy, the Dorchester, the Mayfair, Claridge's, the Berkeley, the Curzon, the Metropole, the Paris-Pullman, the Chelsea, the Astoria, the Rialto, the Plaza, the Prince Charles, the Haymarket, the North British, the Waldorf, the Angus, the Bon Accord, the Crown, the Caledonian, & the Elephant & Castle, & that all monies revenues tips & other proceeds from the running of these high-class establishments are to be paid directly to him at his home address on the occasion of his birthday each year until he attains the age of 131 (one hundred & thirty one). BY ORDER OF DAME KIND (signed).

When Paul looked up from reading this extraordinary document it was to see the old lady pedalling away furiously through the rainbow. Perhaps, though, it was not *through* but UP, for the seven-coloured spokes of the front wheel of her bicycle seemed to leave the ground and take her spinning through bright air. Paul, however, did not notice this. He had turned and was running, running, running down the road for home. He had gone a little further than Peter and it was night by the time he reached his father's house. He stopped and flung his umbrella over the moon before going in. When he told his father about his good luck, and showed him the certificate of ownership of all the hotels, his father said: "Congratulations, lad. I always knew you had it in you."

Poor Pumpkin grew sadder than ever. Not only his father but now his two brothers as well kept hitting him on the head and mocking him. They were successful, you see, and they despised him because he was not.

At last Pumpkin could stand it no longer. In the middle of the night he sneaked away from his father's house. He did not go to his father and announce that he was off into the world to make his fortune because he was sure that a person as silly and full of tears as he was could not possibly have any fortune to make. Consequently he had no gift from his father to aid him in his travels — no walking stick like Peter's to help him when he was tired, no umbrella like Paul's to keep the rain off. As he walked he cried and the tears ran down his face and splashed his throat and chest and feet. He picked some wild flowers to carry but the flowers were beautiful and made him cry the more. It was not just sadness that made Pumpkin cry.

He had not gone more than five or six miles when the old lady on the rainbow bicycle came riding along ringing the silver bell on the handlebars and singing. She slowed down and pedalled beside him. Pumpkin saw that she was wearing little round spectacles, and that one side it was orange glass and the other side indigo. "Good morning, Pumpkin," she said. "Why are you crying?"

"I don't know," said Pumpkin. "I'm always at it."

"You'll cry yourself away," said the old lady. "You'll turn into a puddle."

"I know," said Pumpkin. "It's terrible." And he cried some more at the prospect.

"Crying or not," said the old lady kindly, "you can make your fortune just like your brothers. Now tell me true, what to do for you: ten thousand pounds, your own hotel business, or to learn my art?"

Pumpkin did not hesitate. "Oh," he cried, "I want to learn your art!"

Even as he said the words he felt better. He did not know what the words meant, what the old lady's art was, or why he wanted to learn it. But he did want to learn it, and he always had. As he realised that, Pumpkin stopped crying. His eyes grew bright and he felt happy.

"Pumpkin," said the old lady, "you have answered well." She was still cycling along beside him. When someone is riding a bicycle their feet usually go round and round forwards, like this:

Pumpkin was astonished when he realised that the old lady's feet, encased in little shiny brown shoes, were going round and round *backwards*, like this:

He could not understand how the bicycle went along the road. He looked at the wheels to see which way they were turning, but the rainbow colours of the spokes dazzled his eyes and he could not see properly.

"I am Dame Kind," said the old lady to Pumpkin, "and this is my art: you will be able to change yourself into anything you want, so that if you see a bird in the sky and think to yourself how pleasant it would be to fly and tumble on the wind you have only to spread your arms and flap them a little and you will be a bird, or if you see a fish in the water and think to yourself how pleasant it would be to swim in the cool green places under the lily pads you have only to dive down down down into the pool and you will be a fish, or if you see a flower and think to yourself how pleasant it would be to stand and nod with your head full of seed then you need only lean in the long grass and shut your eyes and you will be a flower."

Pumpkin listened carefully. "That's wonderful," he said. "But how do I learn how to do it?"

"Wonders are many," said the old lady. "Lie down in the road and I will run over you on my bicycle."

"What?" cried Pumpkin.

"You heard," said the old lady.

So Pumpkin lay down in the road and the old lady ran over him on her green bicycle with the white wheels with rainbow spokes, but it didn't hurt at all because the tyres didn't touch the ground and she flew over him some six inches above his body, pedalling furiously and her shiny brown shoes going round and round, around and around, backwards. Then she came bumping back down to earth again on the dusty road. "There," she said, "that's you magicked. Oh larks, I've got a puncture."

And so she had. Pumpkin helped her mend the puncture and then he thanked her for the strange art she had taught him and gave her the flowers he had picked in his walking. He pumped up the mended tyre and the old lady said goodbye. She wheeled her bicycle up to the top of a hill and rode away down the rainbow, going fast, faster, faster, wobbling from one strand of colour to another, red, orange, yellow, green, blue, indigo, violet, indigo, blue, green, yellow, orange, red, orange, yellow, green, blue, indigo, violet, indigo, until Pumpkin could not see which was rainbow and which was old lady, and then she was gone and he could only hear the tinkling of the silver bell on her handlebars, and then that too was gone and Pumpkin was alone.

2

Now it happened that just after Dame Kind disappeared there was a sound of drums and flutes over the hill, and then Pumpkin saw a cloud of dust and flags and banners in the distance coming nearer. All the banners had a lion on them. It was the King and his army on their way to the wars.

As the column of soldiers passed Pumpkin, the King held up his hand for them to stop. He sat down on a milestone, took off his crown, and scratched his head. The soldiers looked at him. Pumpkin looked too. He had never seen the King before.

After about an hour the King put on his crown again. He started practising writing his signature in the dust, using his toecap as a pen. Pumpkin went and stood beside him and this is what he read:

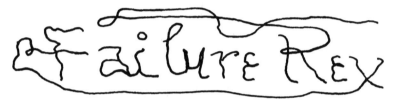

Just like that, in wobbly handwriting.

"*Failure Rex*," said Pumpkin. "What does that mean?"

The King sniffed. He had a long nose. He rested his forefinger along the side of it and looked gloomy. "King Failure," he said. "That's what it means."

"But your name isn't Failure," said Pumpkin.

"It will be," said the King. "It's what the history books will call me when I've lost this war."

"Then don't lose it," said Pumpkin.

The King sighed. "How can I not lose it when I can't even find the enemy?" he demanded. He leant close to Pumpkin's ear. "I've gone and left the maps at home," he hissed.

"Goodness," muttered Pumpkin. "Is that why you're sitting here wasting time and . . . ?"

"Ssssssh!" said the King. A big tear spilled from his left eye and rolled slowly down the side of his nose. Watching its progress, Pumpkin began to cry too. It was an old habit with him. He had too much sympathy.

Then he remembered the powers he had learned from Dame Kind. He brushed away his tears. "Where are the maps then?" he asked the King.

"Under my bed in the brass box painted blue," the King replied. "But it's no good. I need them within twenty-four hours or the war's as good as lost. And my palace is a hundred miles away. No one could get there and back in time."

"I could," said Pumpkin.

The King shook his melancholy head. "Besides, it's dangerous," he added. "There's a dark forest and a deep river and there may well be troops of enemy soldiers hiding here and there."

"Tell your men to rest," Pumpkin told him. "I will bring you the maps before they have time to get to the ends of their dreams."

The King sighed. "If only that was possible," he said. "Do you know, I'd be so pleased I'd give my daughter Possibility in marriage to anyone who could get those maps in time to win the war."

Pumpkin's eyes filled with fresh tears. He had never thought that he would have the chance to marry anyone, let alone a princess. "Is she beautiful?" he asked.

"Very," said the King.

"I won't be long," promised Pumpkin. So saying, he hurried off down the road until he was out of sight. He did not want to make his first attempt at Dame Kind's art where other people could see him, in case it didn't work.

As soon as he reached a quiet place Pumpkin stopped and wondered to himself what was the fastest animal in the land. He saw some hares running in a field. A hare, he thought, that would do very well. A hare was quick and sleek and strong, its legs pumped the ground as it drummed along, its ears lay flat back and its nose nudged and butted at the wind as it sped like a brown arrow or a bolt of furry lightning through green grass, up hill and down dale, never tiring, never stopping, on and on, its haunches like big springs, its paws sure and eager, its eyes clear and unstung by tears even at breakneck paces. . .

The next thing Pumpkin knew he had golden fur on the backs of his hands and his legs were poised ready to hurl him forward in a series of great bounding strides. He sped, he flew, *he was a hare*! He had always been able to imagine what it would be like to be a hare, and the imagining had made him cry with the happiness of it, the long leaping, the running in the sun, the feel of the hard earth under flashing feet, thistles and grasses whizzing by, and the sky streaming about his ears as he dashed towards the horizon. Now he did not only imagine. He *knew*!

Pumpkin the hare ran and ran and ran. The sun sank in the sky and he was still running. At last he came to a great forest.

It was dark inside the forest. The trees grew close together and the bushes and undergrowth made a thick tangled web of branches. Even a hare could not move quickly in such a place.

Right, thought Pumpkin, an end of being a hare — I wish I was a bird! Not just any old bird either, but an eagle, a great soaring golden eagle, able to hurtle down the wind and burn through the sky like a falling star.

And no sooner had he thought it, than he *was* an eagle. Pumpkin was an eagle, high in the air, easily able to wing his way above the great dark forest. He flew fast, he flew high.

But the forest stretched for miles, and Pumpkin's arms began to ache. It was all right being a hare because he was used to running and using his legs, but being an eagle was not so easy because his arms were not used to being wings. He began to drift and lag down the sky and by the time he came to the end of the forest he was very tired.

However, he could not turn back into a hare because he had now to cross a great river. His arms aching so much, Pumpkin wished he was

something without any arms at all, yet something that could go effortlessly through the water.

Of course, *a fish*! He could dive into the river and be a fish. . .

"Help!" cried a little squeaky voice.

Pumpkin looked round. There on the riverbank was a silver mouse-trap, and in the trap a mouse.

Pumpkin's eyes filled with tears. He felt so sorry for it. He could imagine how it felt. . .

Here, he thought to himself, that won't do; with the powers I have now, if I start thinking about this mouse I'll turn into a mouse. So he stopped imagining how the mouse felt, but at the same time he picked open the silver trap so the tiny creature could go free.

"Thanks," squeaked the mouse. It had bright little eyes like sparks. It crossed Pumpkin's mind that he had seen those eyes somewhere before, but he had no time to lose so when the mouse skipped off down the riverbank he dived deftly into the river and turned into a fish. Then he swam through the dark water, all night, sleek and eager, until he came to dry land again, and there was the King's palace in the morning sun.

Taking human form once more, Pumpkin went in and asked to see the Queen. She was kind to him and had the maps fetched from the brass box painted blue. "But tell me," she said, "how did you manage to get here so quickly?"

Pumpkin told her the whole story. He did not want to waste time with questions or with her not believing, so as he told the story he proved what he said was true by changing first into a hare, then into an eagle, finally into a fish before her very eyes. The Queen was delighted. She wanted to keep something to prove that she wasn't dreaming it all, so she pulled out a golden tuft from the fur of Pumpkin the hare, a golden feather from the wing of Pumpkin the eagle, and a golden scale from the side of Pumpkin the fish. These pullings hurt Pumpkin a bit, and he started to cry again. So the Queen gave him a handkerchief of her own to dry his tears. It was a beautiful handkerchief, embroidered with gold. Pumpkin put it in his pocket. Then he tied the maps round his neck in a waterproof otterskin bag, said goodbye to the Queen, and set out on his return journey.

Swimming across the deep river as a fish was not too bad, but flying high above the dark forest as an eagle made Pumpkin tired again. By the time he had reached the far side of it, and turned himself into a hare, he was exhausted. He looked at the sun and saw that he was not late, so after lolloping along for a few miles he made himself a nice grassy nest out of the wind and crouched down on the hillside to rest for a bit.

While Pumpkin was resting a robber came along. The robber saw the big hare and thought to himself that it would make a tasty supper. Poor Pumpkin was so sleepy that he did not notice the robber until it was too late and then the robber was hitting him on the head with a thick stick.

Pumpkin was knocked out, but not killed. He was not killed because the robber was astonished when he saw that the hare had a waterproof otterskin bag tied around its neck, and stopped his hitting. When he undid the bag, the robber found the maps. All of them had the royal seal stamped on them.

Now the robber had passed the King and his army down the road, and he had heard how much the King needed these maps and how he was prepared to give the hand of his daughter in marriage to anyone who could bring them to him in time to win the battle. So he hurried off, leaving Pumpkin (or, as he thought, a half-dead hare) on the hillside. Supper didn't interest him when a Princess was going.

The King jumped up and down when he saw the maps. He marched straight off with them in several directions and won the war. When he returned he took the robber with him in a torchlit triumphal procession back to his palace. He told the Queen that he was going to give their daughter Possibility to this fellow because he had saved the kingdom.

The Queen looked hard at the robber. He did not look at all like Pumpkin, but she supposed he might have changed his form and appearance again and then got stuck, so she said nothing out of politeness.

The Princess Possibility, though, had plenty to say. She was a beautiful girl, with red-gold hair and eyebrows and eyelashes. She had just returned from Finishing School and was in no mood to be married. "You're an old-fashioned tyrant," she told her father. "Nobody gives their daughter away in marriage any more, not these days, and even princesses marry who they like — for love." She glared at the robber.

The robber smirked.

The King put his foot down. "You'll do what I say," he insisted. "A promise is a promise and the wedding will be tomorrow."

3

Pumpkin had terrible dreams. In his dreams he turned into a fox chased by hounds, a grain of corn pecked at by hens, a white dove pursued by two hawks with snapping beaks. The hawks looked like his brothers. He started crying in his sleep, the tears running down his hare's face. But these dreams passed and then he was dreaming of ripples made by the wind at evening on a milky pool. He went on crying because the ripples were so shivery and beautiful. They were like echoes, like laughter, like music. Then in his dream they *were* music, and dancing, and he was dancing, and he was music. . .

Pumpkin woke up. Dame Kind was sitting beside him. Her green bicycle was turned upside down on the ground and she was spinning its rainbow spokes round and round, playing a tune on them with a fiddlestick. When she looked at him he saw that she was not wearing her spectacles. She had bright little eyes like sparks in a chimneyback.

"If you hurry," she said, "we could still have a happy ending."

"The maps!" cried poor Pumpkin, seeing that they were gone. "Oh dear, what shall I do now?"

Dame Kind told him what had happened. "Take this fiddlestick," she said, "and be glad you were blessed with such a kind heart that it couldn't help crying when it saw an insignificant little mouse caught in a trap."

"A fiddlestick?" said Pumpkin. "What can I do with that when I haven't got a fiddle?"

"Play the sunlight," said Dame Kind. "If you can play the sunlight then there will be such music that everyone who hears it will join the dance." Then she climbed on her bicycle and disappeared.

Pumpkin hurried to the King's palace. But when he got there he looked so dusty and dishevelled that the guards would not let him in at the main door, so he had to go round to the kitchen. Once in the kitchen, however, he stood in a shaft of sunlight from a high window and began playing the sunlight with the fiddlestick given to him by Dame Kind. He found it easy enough, being Pumpkin, to imagine that the bright light had shaped itself into a mellow old violin resting between his chin and his cradling hand. The kitchen was filled with glorious music.

The skivvies began to dance, and then the under-maids, and then the maids. The boots danced, and the royal soup-stirrer, and the King's twelve butlers. The pageboys danced, the ladies-in-waiting danced, and then the thirteen cooks and the master chef began to dance also. In and out and up and down they danced, hand in hand, to the music Pumpkin played on the singing sunbeam with the bow given to him by kind Dame Kind. And it was all so sad and happy and lovely and natural and strange that poor Pumpkin began to cry, and the shining tears streamed down his face, and the fiddlestick flashed as it sawed at the light, and the soup bubbled in time to the music, and the plates jumped up and down on the tables with the stamping of the dancers.

Now when the maids and the butlers kept on dancing in and out of the banqueting hall, the King and Queen came down to the kitchen to see what was going on. And the first thing the Queen saw was her handkerchief with the gold embroidery on it, that Pumpkin was using to dry his tears.

She asked Pumpkin to tell them what had happened, and he did. "And you see," he said, "it's that robber who stole the maps who's going to marry the princess."

"Oh no he isn't!" cried Possibility, who had just danced in behind her parents. She stared at Pumpkin from under her red-gold eyelashes. "Do you believe in love at first sight?" she demanded.

"I do now," said Pumpkin.

"So do I," said Possibility.

They both blushed.

Then the King asked Pumpkin to turn into a hare, just to prove that what he had said was true. So Pumpkin turned into a hare.

"Ah," cried the robber, bursting in, "but he could be any old hare, couldn't he, not the one he says got the maps!"

But the Queen had the golden tuft she had taken from Pumpkin's fur and now she leaned forward and it matched his hare's coat absolutely.

Then Pumpkin turned into an eagle, and the Queen found the feather fitted his plumage perfectly.

And then Pumpkin turned into a fish, and the scale fitted too!

The robber saw that the game was up and he turned and ran. He ran and ran, and to tell you the truth he ran so fast that his shadow couldn't keep up with him and he disappeared into thin air and was never seen again.

As for the King and Queen they were over-joyed to welcome the real hero as their son-in-law. So Pumpkin married the Princess Possibility, and they lived happily ever after, although sometimes they have a good cry together. "Just for old times' sake," says Pumpkin, "and to give our eyes a bath."

Tung The Master Mason

Long long ago it was summer in China but it sometimes rained and one day when it did Liu Shan the magistrate discovered that his house had a leaky roof. He sent for the mason, Tung. Tung was young, but he was already a master mason. He set to work to mend the magistrate's roof. The rain stopped, the garden steamed in the sun, the birds were singing all around him but Tung did not listen to them. He liked roofs because he liked to hum and hammer. "Just me and my hammer," he sang to himself, "that's a good song."

Liu Shan had a daughter. Her name was Meng. She was as pretty as a little tea-cup. When the rain stopped she went out walking in her father's garden. She liked to put her nose among the wet flowers. She had a pink nose, like a puppy's; it was not her best feature, but it turned up at the tip and was very serviceable for smelling. Meng walked in the garden as shyly as a shadow.

When Tung saw Meng he fell in love with her. She's so lovely, he thought to himself, I could throw my hammer over the house and leap down into the lily pond, just to celebrate! The sight of her walking in the garden left him wanting to make his hammer sing on all the tiles on Liu Shan's roof. He was sure that there would be a different note from each one and that if he played them for Meng it would add up to a tune. He hammered furiously. The tiles gave cracked noises. The roof was not very musical. Oh Meng, thought Tung, if only you could hear the hammer in my heart! And —

"Love!" he shouted.

And banged.

"*Love!*"

Another bang.

"LOVE!"

The third bang was his last bang. The roof gave way. Tung fell through it into Liu Shan's library. Liu Shan was furious.

"Idiot!" he shouted. "Now when it rains there'll be rain all over my important papers. I'll sue you for damages!"

He chased Tung out into the garden.

Meng came running up. "Oh father," she cried, "don't be cross. Look, he's hurt his finger." She turned to Tung. "Here, let me bind it for you with my scarf," she said kindly.

Tung held out his hand and Meng bound his finger. "You were lucky not to break your neck," she told him.

"My neck?" Tung whispered. "It's my heart that's broken. Oh Meng! When I first saw you walking in the garden —"

"Enough!" roared Liu Shan. "How dare you speak to my daughter like that! You're only a common builder."

Tung drew himself up straight. "A master mason, sir," he said. "At your service."

Liu Shan gnawed his droopy moustaches. "Never again," he snarled, "you can be sure of that. And let go of my daughter's hand, you, you — interloper! And then get out of my garden before I set the leopards on you!"

Tung went. The magistrate's leopards were known to be hungry.

When he got home he went to bed. He stayed there all day and the next day, groaning. On the third day his mother came to him and asked if he wanted to see the doctor when the doctor came by in his dragonboat. Tung shook his head and said that there was no medicine for what he was suffering from.

"Oh dear," said his mother, "is it fatal?"

"Probably," said Tung.

"Is it infectious?" said his mother.

"Er, I don't think so," said Tung.

"We must be grateful for small mercies," sighed his mother. "What is it you're suffering from, son?"

"The magistrate's daughter," said Tung.

"The who's *what?*" said his mother.

"The lovely Meng," said Tung. "I love her, mother. She's — she's like a little magic pagoda in a grove full of blossoms. When she smiles it starts kites up in my heart. When she laughs it's windbells. I want to build a house for her, with a roof of slanting gold, and a lantern burning welcome in every window. A place for her to laugh in, and be at home."

His mother put her hand on his forehead. She thought he must have a fever. "Judge Liu's daughter!" she said. "She wouldn't look at you. Poor folks like us — we live below her eyelevel."

"Meng's not proud," said Tung. "She bound my finger with her silk scarf when I hurt it falling through the roof."

"What next?" cried his mother. "You'll kill yourself if you don't look out. I've always said you were careless."

"Oh I shall die," groaned Tung, "of love!"

"Love?" said his mother. "Chopsticks!"

But Tung went on groaning until his mother believed that he was really dying and offered to do anything if only he would stop.

"Anything?" said Tung.

"Anything," promised his mother.

"Then take a wooden clapper and go and beat it in front of Liu Shan's door until someone comes out," said Tung. "Whoever it is, just tell them that you must see the magistrate himself. And when you're shown in to Liu Shan tell him that Tung the master mason is deep in love with his daughter Meng and wants to marry her."

His mother pulled a face. "They'll never open the door when they see who it is," she said. "Your love for this girl has made a joke of us."

Nevertheless, she took a wooden clapper and went to the magistrate's house. When she got there she started clappering. She clappered and clappered. Her arm ached but she did not stop. Liu Shan's servants leaned out of the windows and shouted at her but she did not stop. She loved her son and she was determined to keep her promise and give his message to the magistrate.

At last Liu Shan could stand it no longer. He flung open his front door. "What do you want?" he bellowed. "You with the wooden clapper, what do you want?"

Tung's mother kept on clappering. "It's no good," she puffed. "I want to see your master. I want to speak to Liu Shan."

"I *am* Liu Shan!" Liu Shan thundered. "I *am* the magistrate. What do you want, woman?"

Tung's mother fell down breathless. She thought her arm was going to come off. At last she managed to say: "Forgive me, your judgeship, I didn't recognise you, what with clappering that clapper. It's hard work, you know."

Liu Shan snorted. "I didn't open my door to chat about clappers," he said. "What is it you want? If it's about your wretched son. . . ."

"O sir," cried Tung's mother, "he won't get up. He stays in his bed all day. Just staring, sir, staring at a bit of silk scarf your daughter was kind enough to bind his finger with when he hurt it. He says he's — begging your pardon — in love with her, sir. It's making him ill. He's right off his nice rice puddings. He's white as a mulberry with the silkworms eating it. Only his silkworms are all love. He loves your Meng, sir. He wants to marry her."

"Marry my daughter?" spluttered Liu Shan. "A common builder and decorator? Out of the question!"

Tung's mother sighed. "There now, I knew you'd say that, sir. I told him you would. Such a pity too. My wrist fairly throbs with all this clappering. But — since you say it's out of the question — and I must say I agree, sir — then I've no choice but to go right back on. . . . I promised him, you see, sir. And I'm sure you'll agree that a Chinese mother's word is her bond."

She swung the wooden clapper.

Liu Shan held up his hand. "Desist," he commanded. "Your son can marry my daughter."

"Tung marry Meng!"

"On one condition," Liu Shan went on. He hesitated a moment, sucking his moustaches, searching for impossibles. "The condition," he said, "is that your son must bring me three gifts in exchange for my daughter's hand in marriage. The first gift is a pearl — *a pearl from the mouth of a dragon*. The second gift is a shell — *the shell of a turtle spirit*. The third gift is a lion — *a lion whose mane was the sun*. If Tung brings me these three things, then he shall marry my daughter Meng."

Tung's mother hurried home. She told her son what the magistrate had said. "It's a lesson he's trying to teach you," she added. "Be content with your place in the world. Ambition gets you nowhere."

Tung jumped out of bed. "Not Nowhere," he cried. "The Western Heaven!"

"What?" said his mother, staring at him.

"The Western Heaven," said Tung. "The land of the Buddha. That's the only place I'm likely to get three gifts like those."

His mother began to cry. "Son, son," she moaned, "you're only a mason. What would a mason do in the land of the Buddha?"

"You're right," agreed Tung, "I am a mason."

He ran to his workbench. "I'll take my mason's hammer," he cried. "My mason's trusty hammer."

He swung the hammer round his head a time or two, then smacked the head of it into his left palm. "Me and my hammer," he said softly, "we make a good song. We'll find the right tune to play in the land of the Buddha, in the Western Heaven."

"Come back! Come back!" called his mother, weeping.

But Tung was gone.

2

It was the winter season. High, high in the mountains, on the way to the Western Heaven, a man was climbing in the sky. It was Tung, the master mason. His coat and boots were tattered. He ate the wind and the rain. He was climbing, climbing, climbing, to the land of the great Buddha, his hammer in his hand, making footholds where no man had been before, cutting his way up from ledge to ledge, leaning in the shouting wind, and all the while in his heart he heard a young girl's laughter — and his hammer sang *Love!*

Tung had been climbing now for nearly six months. It was just as well his work had given him a head for heights for he had just passed the top of the world and reached the first ridge of the sky.

As he did so there was a terrible roar and a dragon appeared before him. It had red eyes and red scaly wings.

"Oh yes," said Tung, as casually as he could. "And who are you?"

"I am the dragon of the lower sky!" the dragon roared.

"I recognise you now," said Tung. "I've seen pictures of you. When they want rain in my village they make a big red dragon just like yourself, only they make it out of wood and paper, and they carry it in a procession. And if it rains, they thank you."

The dragon seemed to like this. He roared and nodded his terrible head. Then a doubt misted his red eyes and he said: "But what if it doesn't rain?"

Tung shrugged. "Then I'm afraid they tear you up," he said.

"RRRRRRRRRR," growled the dragon. "How fickle you humans are. If things don't go just your way —"

"Talking of ways," Tung said boldly, "you're in mine."

"Eh?" said the dragon.

"I want to get past," said Tung.

"Well," said the dragon, "you can't."

"Step aside, dragon," said Tung.

"I won't!" said the dragon. "Dragons don't, you know," he added, as if trying to excuse his bad manners.

Tung puffed out his chest. "Listen, my friend," he said quietly, "do you see this hammer?"

"Hammer?" roared the red dragon of the lower sky. "Hammer your hammer then! I'm not afraid of you or your hammer! What can you do to me? I am the dragon of the lower sky. When I roar, it's thunder all over China!"

"Step aside," said Tung. "I am Tung, the master mason. I have climbed into the Western Heaven. I have come to see the Buddha."

The dragon had been making a noise like a flying orchestra. But now he stopped, coughing and spluttering with surprise. "Did you say the Buddha?" he said.

"I did," said Tung.

"You dare to seek the Buddha?" said the dragon.

"I do," said Tung.

The dragon huffed thoughtfully for a moment. Then he said: "Listen to me, master mason Tung. If I let you pass, will you promise to ask the Buddha a question on my behalf?"

"Certainly," said Tung. "What is the question?"

The dragon used his tail to flick a tear from his red eye. "You must ask the wise Buddha," he said sorrowfully, "why the dragon of the lower sky, who has been perfecting himself for one thousand years, is not allowed to go up into the middle sky."

"Right," said Tung. "I'll ask him that."

"It's just not fair," complained the dragon. "I've done my best, but nothing seems good enough. I've tried and tried, but it's not appreciated. Prejudice, that's what it is! And they have it much better up there in the middle sky, you know. The weather and everything. Much much nicer. You'd think after a thousand years I'd earned the right to a comfortable cloud or two, wouldn't you?"

"I'll ask the Buddha your question, dragon," Tung promised. "Now let me pass."

"Oh yes, of course," said the dragon. "Sorry to keep you gossiping. I'm a talkative old thing, when I get the chance. You wouldn't think it to look at me, would you, what with all these red scales and roaring and all? Well, good luck to you, Tung! And don't forget my question."

"I won't," said Tung. "Goodbye."

Tung's hammer was not much use to him now. He stuck it in his belt. He climbed through clouds. He waded through wind. The sun was hanging round his legs. He was nearing the middle sky.

"Oh Meng, Meng," he thought to himself, "I wish I could send you a letter postmarked Heaven. I would say: Dear Meng, Here I am walking through all the colours of the rainbow in a cloud with a blue floor, and it is very nice but nowhere near as lovely as where you are smiling. And yours sincerely, and then three Xs, and a little PS saying —"

His thoughts were interrupted by a dreadful sneezing and wheezing. Looking round, he saw a turtle spirit emerge from a wet cloud.

Tung and the turtle spirit stared at each other for a moment, then —

"All right, all right," wheezed the turtle spirit, speaking slowly and asthmatically, "no need to be polite is there? No need to say good morning how-do-ye-do to the likes of me, eh? I know you despise me, of course. I can see it in your eyes. You're thinking: He's not much. He's only some old turtle spirit hanging about in the middle sky of the Western Heaven. Well, let me warn you — I'm not as soft and silly as I look. In fact, this shell of mine's as hard as iron, and if I was to drop a bit sharpish on your head right now you'd go down, down, down like a falling star and break every bone in your body. I say! My word! What are you going to do with that nasty horrible hammer?"

Tung was holding the hammer high over his head. "Let me pass, turtle spirit," he commanded. "I am Tung, the master mason. I am on my way to see the Buddha."

"The Buddha, is it?" wheezed the turtle spirit. Then he added in a crafty voice, "If I let you pass, will you do something for me?"

"What?" said Tung.

"Will you ask the Buddha a question?" said the turtle spirit.

"What question?" said Tung.

"Oh I knew you would!" wheezed the turtle spirit. "You've got kind hands, despite that dreadful hammer. You ask the Buddha, in his wisdom, to tell you why it is that the turtle spirit of the middle sky, who has been busy perfecting himself for two thousand years, isn't allowed to go on up into the upper sky. You ask him that." He paused to wipe his runny nose. "I know I'm not as strong as I might be," he admitted. "It's this dratted asthma. The climate doesn't suit me a bit. But I've been perfecting my —"

"I'll ask the Buddha your question," promised Tung.

"You *are* a pal," cried the turtle spirit. "Thanks very much. What did you say your name was? Tung, wasn't it? Well, Tung, I'll do something for you. I'll write your name with cloud so your friends down there on earth can see it. It'll be a sort of advertisement for you."

Tung smiled. "Write: Tung loves Meng," he said.

"Tung loves Meng," repeated the turtle spirit. He sighed. "How romantic," he said. "Yes, I'll do it. With a heart and arrows."

"Thanks," said Tung. "Goodbye."

"Goodbye," said the turtle spirit. "And don't forget my question."

Tung went on his way.

On and on he went.

And up and up he went.

But the higher he climbed, the deeper he fell —
in love. The air was thin, but in thin air everywhere he saw and heard his love, the lovely
Meng. She beckoned in blue and wore the sun
like a brooch. Tung's heart was on fire with her.
He was forgetting what he had come for.

"I am Tung," he said to himself. "I am Tung,

the master mason. I have come to mend the roof of the Western Heaven. One or two stars need repairing, isn't that it? The Buddha knows I've the cunningest hammer in all China. He wants me to mend the moon. I have to put a cowl on the sun to stop it smoking. It's only a half-hour's work, at the usual rates, for a master mason like me."

Now, as Tung was losing his memory, what with the altitude and his love for Meng, the sky started to throb and the clouds turned into music. All at once it was neither summer nor winter. All at once it was neither China nor anywhere else.

Tung the master mason had entered the halls of the Buddha! He stood before the lotus throne at the highest peak of Heaven.

"I am the Buddha," said the Buddha. "I am the Buddha. You are Tung. Why does Tung come to the Buddha?"

Tung held his head. "Oh Meng, oh Meng," he cried.

"Answer me!" commanded the Buddha. "Man must answer the Buddha when the Buddha asks. Why have you come, O Tung of the mighty hammer?"

Tung could not think straight. "I don't know," he stammered. "I've forgotten. No. I'm trying to remember. It's because of the wind-bells. I love. I love Meng. There were precious things I was to ask you for. Or was it — to ask you? Precious things. Meng! I've forgotten them." He shook his head. Then: "No," he cried. "It's coming back. I remember now. The first thing —"

"Yes?" said the Buddha kindly.

"The poor red dragon of the lower sky," said Tung. "He's been perfecting himself for a thousand years, you know. Why can't he go up into the middle sky?"

"I like your question and will answer it," said the Buddha. "The dragon cannot go up into the middle sky because he has two pearls in his mouth. All the other dragons have only one. If our friend spits out the second pearl, then he will go up into the middle sky."

"O Buddha," cried Tung gratefully, "I will tell him."

"The second thing?" demanded the Buddha.

Tung rubbed his eyes with the backs of his hands. "I wish I could concentrate," he moaned. "It must be the air, or the height, or the light, or something. Oh Meng, Meng, I wish I was just on the roof of your father's house again, looking down at you in the cool of the garden. I wouldn't bang or sing. I'd just sit quiet and watch you watching the butterflies. Oh Meng, I would build you a house of butterflies, with a rose for a door, and tiny peacocks going out and in — "

The Buddha said: "The second question, Tung!"

"The turtle spirit of the middle sky," Tung cried, "he has been working away perfecting himself for two thousand years. And he has asthma,

Sir, and the climate doesn't suit him. Why can't he go up into the upper sky?"

"Your question honours you," said the Buddha. "I will answer it. The turtle spirit cannot ascend because his shell is too hard. If he could get rid of it then he could easily come into the upper sky. And it's the weight of that shell that gives him his asthma. Without it, he'd be right as rain."

"O Buddha," said Tung gratefully, "I will tell him."

There was a silence. Then the Buddha said: "Have you no more to ask me?"

Tung shook his head doubtfully. "Er, no," he said. "That's all. That's all I can remember."

"That is good," said the Buddha. "It is good that you have asked me things on behalf of other creatures, and not for yourself. Because you have done this, O Tung, I shall make you a gift. I think that it will prove to be a very useful gift."

He clapped his hands and a lion appeared from behind the sun. The lion's mane was all fiery and wiry, made out of twisted strands of sunlight.

"Ride on the lion's back," said the Buddha, "and your way down from the Western Heaven will be easy."

Tung thanked the Buddha and mounted the lion whose mane was the sun. He rode out of heaven on the lion's back. He rode and rode and rode, down and down, and down. He gave the Buddha's answers to the turtle and the dragon.

The turtle was so happy that he gave his shell to Tung after Tung had helped him to remove it, tapping with his hammer, gently, gently, as a master mason can. The dragon was so happy, he gave his tooth to Tung — the tooth which was a pearl and which kind Tung removed for him, as simply as a dentist. And Tung rode on down on the lion whose mane was the sun, and all his thought was: *Meng!*

3

When Meng met Tung and saw that he was safe she burst into tears. Then she saw what he had brought back with him from the Western Heaven.

"O Tung, O Tung, I love you!" she cried, dancing round him for joy. "Daddy will have to let me marry you now because you've brought back just the three things he asked for — the precious impossible things he was sure you could never ever get — *a pearl from the mouth of a dragon, the shell of a turtle spirit, a lion whose mane was the sun.* Oh what a lovely likely lion it is, too!" She stroked the lion's neck. "Does he bite?" she asked.

"Not if you handle him firmly but kindly and give him plenty of tea," said Tung. "Do that, and let him have three lumps of sugar in the tea, and he'll probably dance at our wedding."

Liu Shan the magistrate came striding up. He saw at a glance that Tung had succeeded in his quest for the three impossible gifts. He saw also that his daughter and the young master mason were deeply in love.

"Young man," he admitted, "I misjudged you. I take back everything I ever said against you. Plainly you are a remarkably gifted person. Very promising. Very promising indeed. I'd say you have a great future. I shall be pleased to have you for a son-in-law." He paused, twisting his moustaches. "Tell me," he added, "how did you manage to do it?"

Tung scratched his head with his hammer. "I don't know, sir," he said slowly. "I suppose I was so in love that it — it just happened. Luck."

"I wouldn't call it luck!" said Liu Shan.

"Neither would I," added Tung's mother, who had just come running up on hearing the good news of her son's safe return from the land of the Buddha. "Oh he's modest, your judgeship. Luck indeed!"

Meng put her pretty head close to Tung's and whispered in his ear. "Was it luck, Tung?"

"I don't know," Tung whispered back. "Perhaps luck is something that happens to you when you love someone so much that you stop worrying about yourself and then things go right for you? Perhaps it was just something to do with my hammer? It's always been a lucky sort of hammer. And I'm only a mason, a master mason. I'm not much good at understanding things. But — oh Meng, I love you! What do you think?"

The Witches Who Stole Eyes

There was once a boy called Tom Fortune whose mother died and father died, leaving him all alone and having to seek his own way in the world. He was a brave boy, not afraid of anyone or anything, so after he had cried for his poor mother and cried for his poor father he did not cry for himself, but set out instead with a red pack on his back and green leather boots on his feet, marching up hill and down dale looking for someone who would hire him. His head was high and his eyes were bright and he sang a song as he marched. This is how the song went:

"I'm Tom, Tom, Tom!
I'm Tom, Tom, Tom!
Tom's not afraid
Of ANY — ONE!

I'm Tom, not Tim!
Tom! Tom! Not Tim!
Tom's not afraid
Of ANY — THING!"*

It was a fine song and he sang it in a loud proud voice and it certainly cheered him up although the rhymes were not very good. In this way he marched for miles until he came to a country he did not know.

The first thing Tom Fortune saw in the country he did not know was a little squat cottage that stood on the edge of a deep dark forest. In the doorway of the cottage sat an old man. He was bent and thin, with no teeth and empty black holes where his eyes should have been. He had a long beard like a ragged sleeve.

Tom could hear goats bleating in the tumbledown shed beside the cottage, and as he stood watching, flapping his red pack up and down on his back, the old man suddenly gazed up blindly at the sun, twisting his beard in his hands, and called out:

"Sorry, goats, sorry! I wish I could take you to pasture. But I can't, because I can't see, and I've no one to send with you."

Tom chafed his green boots. "Send me!" he cried. "I'll take your goats to pasture, uncle. And I'll do all the work for you as well."

"Who's that?" demanded the old man, shivering with fright.

"My name is Tom Fortune," said Tom, and he stepped forward and told the old man his story.

When Tom had finished he noticed that the old man had been so nervous during the telling that he had tied his beard in knots. He wondered what the old man was frightened of. However, he said nothing, but helped the old man undo the knots.

"Thank you, Tom," said the old man, when they had done. He thought for a minute or two, rubbing his hands together as though he was washing them. Then he took a deep shuddery breath and said:

"All right, my boy, you can work for me, and welcome. The first thing you have to do is drive my goats to pasture."

"That's easy, uncle," said Tom. He cut a white stick from the willow tree, to drive the goats with. Then he skipped about busily in his green boots, letting the noisy creatures out of their shed.

The old man started twisting his beard again.

"Not so fast, not so fast, Tom Fortune!" he called in his trembly voice. "Before you go off I want to warn you about something."

Tom puffed out his chest. "I'm not scared of anything or anyone," he boasted.

"Maybe you *should* be scared of some things," said the old man. He nodded to himself once or twice, as though he had said something important. Then he said, "Listen, whatever you do, don't let the goats go into the green glade in the forest."

"Why not?" said Tom.

"Because," said the old man, "there are three witches who live there, and if you let the goats go into the green glade the witches will come and send you to sleep and then they will steal your eyes as they stole mine."

Tom tossed his head proudly. "I don't believe in witches," he scoffed.

The old man said nothing. He just pointed with his stick-like fingers to the places where his eyes should have been.

A shiver made Tom's spine tingle. "Well," he promised, "I'll be careful, uncle. Don't worry, I shan't let anyone steal my eyes."

Then he drove the goats out of the yard and into the safe and sunny meadows that lay below the deep dark forest, singing his song as he went:

"I'm Tom, Tom, Tom!
I'm Tom, Tom, Tom!
Tom's not afraid
Of any — one!

I'm Tom, not Tim!
Tom! Tom! Not Tim!
Tom's not afraid
Of any — thing!"

Soon the goats were munching the long grass and dandelions were hanging out of their mouths.

2

The next day, and the day after that, Tom Fortune took the goats out to the meadows. But the day after the day after that was a very hot day, the sun glaring like a big red eye in the bright blue sky and the ground all cracked and dusty underfoot, and Tom thought to himself:

"How cool it looks in the glade over there in the forest. . . . And the pasture is better besides — long, lush green grass, and daisies, and dandelions. . . . The poor goats would love it!"

He had not forgotten the old man's warning, but he was almost ashamed to be remembering it. "Why should I be afraid of witches," he thought, "when I don't even believe that there are such things?" He strutted up and down in his green boots, kicking at the ground, trying to make his mind up what to do. At last he was decided. He cut himself three long bramble shoots for luck, stuck them in his cap, and drove the goats straight into the forest, through the cool shadows under the trees, into the rich green glade. The nannygoats ran bleating with pleasure when they saw and smelt the good grass, and the billygoats put down their heads and butted each other to get at the best bits, but soon they had all settled down together to crop and munch contentedly. Tom Fortune sat down on a stone in the shade.

He had not been sitting there long when he looked round and saw that a girl was standing beside him. Tom rubbed his eyes. He had not seen her come walking through the trees. It was as if she had appeared out of sunlight. The girl was dressed in white linen from head to foot, but her hair was black and glossy as a raven's wing and she had eyes like blackberries glistening with dew.

"Good morning, Greenboots," she said.

"Good morning," said Tom, looking somewhere else. She was the most beautiful girl he had ever seen.

The girl smiled. "My name is Beauty," she said.

"Hello Beauty. My name is Tom," said Tom.

"Hello Tim," said Beauty.

Tom frowned. "Not Tim," he said. "Tom."

"Are you sure?" demanded Beauty.

"Of course I'm sure," said Tom. "T.O.M. Tom. That's me."

"Well, you don't much look like a Tom and that's certain," said Beauty. "If ever I saw a Tim — it's you! T.I.M. Tim. Short for *timid*, I daresay."

Tom went red in the face and was just going to say something angry when Beauty took an apple from her sleeve and went on quickly: "I expect you didn't know that over there, deep in the forest, there's an apple tree, and that the apples that grow on the tree are the sweetest apples in all the world. And I'll tell you why you didn't know. Because you're scared to go in the forest, aren't you, Tim? And even if you did go, you'd be scared to eat one of the apples!"

Tom stamped his foot. "My name is TOM!" he shouted. "And I'm not afraid of anything!"

Beauty smiled sweetly and held out the apple to him. "Go on then," she murmured. "Eat it."

Tom took the apple in his hand. He longed to sink his teeth into it, and prove Beauty wrong, but something made him stop. He noticed that although the apple *looked* good it did not shine in the sun as you would expect a red apple to shine. Also, it felt soft and heavy in his grasp.

Tom rubbed the apple suspiciously against his cheek. It had no smell at all. "Did you pick it just for me?" he asked.

"Yes," said Beauty.

"Why?" said Tom.

Beauty smiled again. "Because you have such lovely blue eyes," she said.

Tom blinked. So that was it! There *were* such things as witches. This girl was a witch — and she was after his eyes. If he ate the apple he would surely fall asleep as the old man had warned, and then Beauty would steal his eyes.

He shook his head. "No thanks," he said, "I don't want the apple. My master has an apple tree in his garden all dripping with apples better than yours. I've eaten my fill." And drawing back his arm he threw the poisoned apple as far into the forest as he could.

Beauty was angry, but she still made her face smile. "Very well," she purred. "Now I *know* that your name is Tim!"

And she walked off into the forest, singing a bitter little song.

About an hour passed. Tom Fortune sat dreaming in the shade, watching the goats champ and munch. He saw a buzzard high in the blue sky overhead, like a full-stop scratched on the sun. Then he noticed that another girl was standing at his elbow. She was more beautiful than the first girl. She had golden hair and was dressed in green. In her right hand she held a white rose.

"Good morning, Greenboots," she said.

"Good morning," said Tom.

The girl smiled. "My name is Truth," she said.

"Hello Truth. My name is Tom," said Tom.

"Hello Tim," said Truth.

Tom took a deep breath. "Not Tim," he said. "Tom."

"No," said Truth, "I don't think so. If you were a real Tom you wouldn't be frightened of me. And you are frightened, aren't you?"

"Not in the least," said Tom, although he was.

The girl held up the white rose. "In that case," she murmured, "I suppose you won't be afraid to smell how sweet this rose is. I picked it in the forest just for you."

Oh yes, thought Tom, and if I do smell your rose I will fall asleep and you will steal my eyes! So he shook his head, and said: "No thank you, Truth. My master has even sweeter roses in his garden. I have smelled all the roses I want."

Truth's face went dark with rage when Tom refused the rose. She threw the flower to the ground and crushed it with her heel. "Please yourself, *Tim*," she muttered, and stalked off into the forest without another word.

Noon came and went. Tom Fortune watched the goats and played with the brambles he had stuck in his cap. It was very hot and he would dearly have liked to stretch out in the shade and enjoy a nap, but he did not dare do this in case the witches came and stole his eyes. He was not surprised when a third girl appeared at his side. She was the youngest and most beautiful of them all. She had long red hair and was dressed in a dark gown.

"Good afternoon, Greenboots," she said.

"Good afternoon," said Tom.

This girl did not smile. Her eyes and lips were sad. "My name is Innocence," she said.

"Hello Innocence. My name is Tom," said Tom.

"Hello Tom," said Innocence.

Tom Fortune was so pleased that she had called him by his right name that he forgot to be suspicious when Innocence took a silver comb from her dark sleeve, saying: "What a handsome boy you are, Tom Greenboots. But your hair is all sticky and untidy with the heat. Lie back and let me comb it for you!"

Innocence came closer, her lips still sad, the silver comb in her outstretched hand. "Oh Tom," she murmured, "such pretty blue eyes you have! Such pretty little sweet little lovely little nice blue eyes!"

Tom jumped to his feet before she could plunge the silver comb into his hair. Snatching up his cap he took one of the bramble shoots from it and smacked at Innocence's hand.

The witch — for, of course, she *was* a witch — gave a high-pitched scream. Because Tom had dared to strike her all her powers were gone. She began to cry, for she could not move from the spot.

"Beauty!" she shrieked. "Beauty! Truth! Sister witches! Help! Help me!" Her voice was like that of a hare caught fast in a trap.

Tom Fortune hardened his heart to her crying, remembering that she would have picked his eyes out if he had given her half a chance. Quickly he twined the bramble round and round her wrists.

Beauty and Truth came running out of the dark forest. When they saw what Tom had done to their sister they began to beg him to unbind her and set her free, promising him anything if he would.

"Unbind her yourselves!" said Tom.

"We can't!" cried Beauty.

"Our skin is softer than mortal skin," explained Truth. "The bramble would prick and tear us!"

All the same, when they saw that Tom was determined to keep their sister prisoner they went to her aid, trying to unpick the bramble that bound her. As soon as they did that, Tom sprang upon them and struck them both on the hands with the other bramble shoots. Then he tied them up with the brambles.

"You wicked horrible Greenboots!" wailed Beauty.

"You cruel unfeeling mortal!" howled Truth.

"Just wait till we're free!" screamed Innocence. "We'll scratch out your eyes, you miserable boy!"

Tom shook his head. "How dare you say I'm horrible to stop your tricks?" he demanded. "Witches who steal eyes deserve all they get!"

And, so saying, he ran home helter-skelter through the forest to tell his master the news.

"Uncle!" he cried. "Come with me!" And he grabbed the old man by the arm.

"Where are we going?" asked the old man in confusion.

"You'll see!" promised Tom. "Yes," he added, "you'll see all right, because *we're going to get back your eyes!*"

3

Tom Fortune led his master to the green glade where he had left the three witches. They were still there, weeping and wailing and trying to break their bramble bonds.

Tom went up to Beauty. "Now," he said, "you tell me where my master's eyes are and I'll set you free. But if you don't tell me . . . then I'll throw you in that stream over there!"

Beauty shook with fright. "I don't know where his eyes are," she said sulkily.

"Right," said Tom, his face grim. "Into the water you go!"

Now witches are like cats only more so. The thought of being pitched into the stream filled Beauty's heart with terror. She knew that she must drown.

"Don't throw me in, Greenboots," she begged. "Please, please, dear kind generous Greenboots, don't throw me in the water! I'll give you your master's eyes!"

Tom undid her bonds and followed warily as the witch led him to a cave in the forest.

The cave was full of eyes! There were big eyes and little eyes, bright eyes and weary eyes, blue eyes, brown eyes, hazel eyes and amber eyes, hawk eyes and bat eyes, eyes as sharp as needles and eyes oozing tears, all sorts and shapes and sizes and colour and condition of eyes.

Beauty picked up a pair of eyes from the pile, and gave them to Tom. Tom ran back to the old man, dragging the witch behind him. Then he set the eyes in his master's head.

"Can you see, uncle? Can you see?" he cried excitedly, skipping round and round him.

"Yes!" shouted the old man. "I can see! But all I can see is mice and shrews and voles and moonlight! Too-whit! Too-whoo!" And he stretched out his scraggy arms and rocked to and fro on his heels making hooting noises.

The witches laughed wickedly. Tom grew very angry.

"These are not my master's eyes!" he cried. "You gave me owl's eyes!" And he seized Beauty by her long black hair and threw her into the water, where she drowned.

"Now," Tom said to Truth. "You fetch my master's eyes this minute or it will be the worse for you!"

The witch began to make excuses and say she did not know where they were, but when Tom Fortune seized her by her golden hair and dragged her through the forest to the cave where the eyes were heaped she went in to the pile and chose another pair and brought them back to him. Tom ran to the old man and set the new eyes in his head.

"Can you see, uncle? Can you see?"

"Yes!" cried the old man. "But oh dear, oh

dear, all I can see is snow and wastes and woods and sledges and — *ooooow!* OOOOOOW! I *would* like a fresh young lamb to eat!"

"Wolf's eyes!" said Tom grimly. And he caught Truth and threw her into the water, where she drowned too.

"Now," Tom said to Innocence. "You tell me where my master's eyes are! And no tricks, or it's in the stream you go to join your sisters!"

At this, the witch began to wring her hands and moan, saying she did not know where the old man's eyes were — but Tom Fortune would take no nonsense. He dragged her to the cave and told her to fetch them quickly. Innocence went in to the pile and chose another pair and gave them to him without a word.

Tom ran back to the old man and set the new eyes in his head.

"Can you see, uncle? Can you see?"

"Yes!" cried the old man. "But all I can see is reeds and water and pebbles and old boots and lots of little fishes I want to gobble up!"

"Pike's eyes!" said Tom.

He was so furious at having been deceived three times that he seized Innocence by her long red hair and dragged her to the water's edge.

"Spare me!" she pleaded. "Spare me, Tom Greenboots, and I promise that this time I will bring you your master's own eyes without fail!"

Tom took pity on her. He remembered that,

after all, she was the only one who had called him by his proper name. Hand in hand they went back together through the forest to the cave and Innocence went in to the pile and drew out a pair of eyes that were right at the bottom, underneath all the others.

"These are your master's eyes," she said, giving them to Tom.

So Tom ran back to the old man and set the eyes in his head. This time the old man clapped his hands for joy.

"I can see!" he cried, dancing round and round on his spindly bent legs. "Yes, these are my eyes . . . A slight squint in the left, perfect vision in the right! Oh, it's good to have them back! Hurrah! I can see again at last!"

Tom turned to the witch Innocence.

"Thank you," he said.

"That's all right, Tom Greenboots," said Innocence. "I'm only sorry they were ever stolen. I'm only sorry I was ever a witch to do such things. I'll never never do it again!"

Then Tom Fortune and his master went back together through the forest to their little cottage, where they lived happily ever after. Every day Tom took the goats out to pasture and brought them home and milked them. The old man made the milk into cheese, and they both ate the cheese.

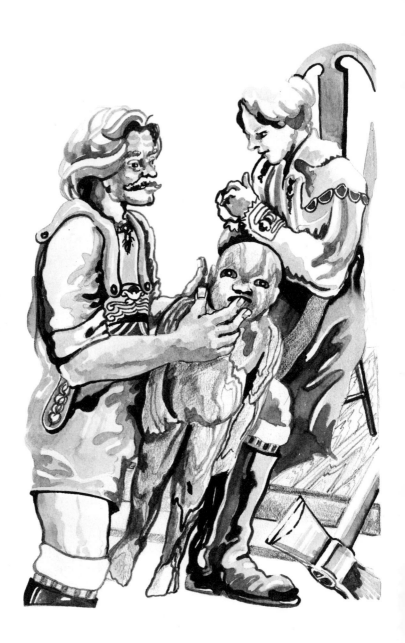

The Wooden Baby

Krog was a woodcutter. He lived with his wife Mog in a green cottage on the edge of a black forest. They were very poor. Every morning Krog went off to work with his bright axe over his shoulder. He wore big boots and trousers made of moleskin. Mog stayed at home and spun flax. She wore a bonnet and sang hymns as she turned the spindle. When Krog came back every evening at sunset they sat down to dinner. All they had to eat was turnips. They had turnip soup, turnip chops, and turnip jelly. It was horrible and they were very thin.

One night Mog put down her wooden spoon and said: "I wish we had a baby."

"A baby?" said Krog. "We couldn't afford it. We haven't enough to eat ourselves. How could we feed a baby?"

Mog sighed. "I suppose you're right," she said. "All the same, I'd like one."

The next night she said the same thing. And the next night. And the one after that. Krog was a patient man, so he did not complain or get angry. But when Mog started talking about babies in the morning too, he grew sick of the subject. There were not enough turnips to have breakfast — dinner was their only meal — and he hated making commonsensical remarks on an empty stomach.

One morning, after a whole week of listening to his wife talking about babies, Krog was out as usual chopping wood in the forest when he saw a tree that looked like an old man. It was black and bent, with long twisting roots that poked up through the cracked earth like dirty toenails. This gave him an idea. He stopped and stared at the tree, wiping the sweat from his face. Then he turned back to his log, cut it neatly in half, stripped off the bark and began slicing and chopping at the white wood. He shaped the end until it was round and smooth like a baby's head. He gave it a body, and arms, and legs. He trimmed the roots to make them look like fingers and toes. When he had finished it looked just like a real baby.

Krog took it up tenderly under his arm and ran home. Mog was sitting in the porch with her bonnet on, spinning flax and singing hymns. Krog held the wooden baby behind his back so that she would have a surprise.

"Heavens," said Mog, "what are you doing home so early? You'll lose your job!"

"Never mind that," said Krog. "Look what I've got!"

And he held it up for her to see.

His wife was so amazed she had to take her bonnet off to let the air to her head. "A baby!" she cried.

"A wooden baby," said Krog. "Well, do you want it?"

Mog clapped her hands. "Yes, yes, of course I do," she said. She took the baby from him, hurried indoors, and wrapped it in the tablecloth. Krog went back to the forest to work, pleased that she was pleased. When he reached the place where he had left his axe he noticed that the tree like an old man seemed to be shaking its head at him in the wind. But he ignored it.

Meanwhile, Mog was sitting in the parlour, rocking the baby in her arms and singing a song to it:

> *"Lullaby, hushaby,*
> *Little wooden baby boy.*
> *When you wake, my pet, my sweet,*
> *You shall have some food to eat.*
> *Lullaby, hushaby."*

All at once the wooden baby started to wriggle about in the tablecloth. It kicked its legs. It turned its shiny head. Then it began to scream and shout.

"Food!" it bellowed. "Food! Food! Food! I want food to eat!"

Its voice was so loud that the words cracked every piece of crockery on the dresser. The cups crashed to the tiled floor, leaving only their handles swinging on the hooks.

Mog did not know whether to laugh or cry. "Oh dear," she said. "I didn't mean it. I thought that you wouldn't really want anything, being made of wood, that is. I can't —"

"FOOD!" roared the wooden baby. And this time its shout shattered the windowpane and made the kettle explode.

"Sshh, sshh," soothed Mog. "I'll get you something, my poppet. Just wait a minute. It won't take a moment. I'll make you some nice turnip porridge, how's that?"

The baby glared at her. Its face was very red and it had eyes like knots. It did not look as though it much fancied the idea of turnip porridge. But it lay quietly enough while Mog lit the fire and stirred the pot.

When the porridge was ready, Mog wiped her hands on her apron, took her own spoon from the drawer and began feeding the baby. The fat lips gobbled greedily. The throat gurgled as the porridge slid down. When it was all gone the baby belched.

"Pardon!" said Mog.

The baby looked at her. It took a deep breath.

"Food!" it shouted. "Food! Food! Food! I want food to eat!"

"Goodness," said Mog, "the poor thing *is* hungry. Never mind, my jewel. I'll get you something as quick as I can."

There were no turnips left, except those for Krog's supper. So Mog rushed out of the house with a pail in her hand, ran down the road, found a cow in a field, milked it, and hurried back. The baby did not give her time to pour the milk into a jug. As soon as it saw her coming it reached out one greedy hand and grabbed the pail. It drank all the milk in one gluttonous gulp, creamy suds running down its chin. Then it gave a terrible belch that made the house shake and dust fly out of the cushions.

"Pardon?" said Mog, doubtfully.

The baby looked at her. It rolled its eyes. It took a deep breath. . . .

"No!" cried Mog. "Don't shout! Please, please don't shout again. I'll get you something. I will. I promise. Only —"

"FOOD!" roared the baby. "FOOD! FOOD! FOOD! I WANT FOOD TO EAT!"

The shouts were so loud they made the chimney fall off. A crow that had been nesting there was so frightened that all its feathers dropped out. It flapped away into the forest, bald and squawking like a chicken.

Now Mog was a proud woman, and although she had always been poor she had never borrowed in her life. But she had to do something to meet the wooden baby's enormous appetite. So she ran down the road to her nearest neighbour and begged for a loaf of bread. When she got back the baby was asleep. It lay on its back, snoring. The noise was like thunder. Mog crept in and put the loaf on the table. Then she went out into the yard to draw water from the well to set on the fire for soup.

All the flowers in the garden were trembling in time with the baby's snores. Suddenly they stopped. Mog looked nervously at the house. The baby had woken up.

"FOO —!"

The ear-shattering shout broke off before the word was finished. The baby had evidently seen the loaf. Mog smiled to herself.

"Such a sweet little thing really," she murmured.

But when she went back into the parlour to make breadcrumbs for the soup she found that the loaf was gone. "The sweet little thing" had not just *seen* it. It had eaten it! The whole loaf! And, what was worse, the baby was growing fatter and fatter and hungrier and hungrier with every tick of the clock. Before Mog's eyes, it started eating the tablecloth, stuffing it into its mouth and chewing, chewing, chewing. Its eyes rolled. Its cheeks bulged. With a huge gulp it swallowed the lot.

"Mercy on us!" cried Mog. "Will you never stop?"

The baby looked at her. It was now as big as a barrel. It opened its mouth to shout.

"Hush!" Mog pleaded. "Don't ask for more! You've eaten all I have!"

The baby blinked. It peeped through its chubby wooden fingers at her. This time it did not shout. But its quiet voice was more dreadful than its loud voice. "That's right," it said. "I've eaten all you have — and now I'm going to eat you too!"

And it did. Before Mog could move the baby jumped on her and gobbled her up. In a minute all that was left of her was her clogs, her bonnet, and her hymn-book, lying on the floor beside the big fat wooden baby.

2

Krog came home early from the forest. As he unlatched the little green gate he heard a terrible bellow from the cottage.

"Food! Food! Food! Food! Food! *I want food to eat!*"

Krog dropped his axe and ran into the parlour. The baby was trying to eat the carpet. He hardly recognised it — it had grown so fat.

"Help!" cried Krog. He looked round for his wife. "Where's your mummy? Mog! Mog! Where are you, Mog?"

The baby stood up. Its tiny legs could scarcely support it. Its belly was like a small mountain.

"No use shouting for mummykins," it said softly. "I've eaten her."

"You've *what?*" said Krog.

"Eaten her," said the baby. "And now I'm going to eat you too!"

And it did. Before Krog could move the baby jumped on him and gobbled him up. All that was left of him was his big boots and his moleskin trousers.

The wooden baby was still hungry. There was nothing left to eat in the cottage, so it went out and waddled off down the road to the village. It could not walk very fast because it was so fat. Before long it met a little girl. She was riding along on a new bicycle, ringing the bell and enjoying the swishing sound of the tyres on the warm road.

The baby stopped and the girl ran into it. It was so fat she just bounced off. She picked up her bicycle and glared crossly. She was a very rude little girl, with a curl in the middle of her forehead.

"Hey, Fatty," she said, "whatever have you been eating to get a tum like that?"

The wooden baby rolled its eyes and answered:

> "*I've eaten, I've gobbled:*
> *Some turnip porridge,*

One pail of milk,
One loaf of bread,
A tablecloth,
My mummy, my daddy —
And I'll eat you too!"

And it did. Before the little girl could move the baby sprang on her and gobbled her up, bicycle and all. She put the brakes on as she went down its throat, but that could not save her.

The wooden baby went on its way. Before long it met a farmer bringing a load of hay from a meadow. It stood in the middle of the road, and the horse had to stop.

The farmer leaned down and cracked his whip. "Out of my way, Puffy Guts!" he shouted.

The wooden baby just blinked at him, licking its lips. Then it began its song again:

"I've eaten, I've gobbled:
Some turnip porridge,
One pail of milk,
One loaf of bread,
A tablecloth,
My mummy, my daddy,
A girl with a bicycle —
And I'll eat you too!"

The farmer snorted. "Oh no you won't!" he said. "It would take more than a fat freak like you to — "

But the baby swallowed him before he could finish the sentence, and the horse and cart as well. All this lot took a bit of eating, but the baby was getting hungrier and hungrier. The strange thing was that the more it ate the greedier it got. To start with, it had not liked things like Mog's bonnet and Krog's boots, but now it was ready for anything. When it had finished the horse it gave a belch like a cannon going off. Then it continued on its way.

Just down the road was a man driving pigs home from market. The wooden baby did not stop to say hello. It simply opened its mouth and sucked them all in.

The baby was now beginning to feel a bit sick. Its tummy rumbled. Its eyes were popping. It could not walk straight. But when it saw a shepherd in a field rounding up his sheep it thought to itself, "Another little snack won't do any harm." So it gobbled them up too: the sheep, the shepherd, and even the sheep dog, who was called Mungo and went down the baby's throat wagging his tail and making the horrible creature cough and splutter.

The wooden baby staggered on, its body all swollen and aching with what it had eaten. There really was no room for any more — but the baby was so greedy it could not help wanting more.

"Food!" it chanted. "Food! Food! Food! *I want food to eat!*"

Its voice was not loud and shattering now, because its stomach was full up. The people and things it had swallowed whole rattled about inside it as it waddled along.

3

Now, on the outskirts of the village, in a house with a thatched roof and a twisted chimney, lived an old woman called Mother Bunch. Mother Bunch had a face like a potato. She wore a man's cap and was not afraid of anyone or anything. People said she was a witch.

Mother Bunch was out in her garden hoeing cabbages when she saw what looked like a hippopotamus walking down the road. It was not a hippopotamus. It was the wooden baby. She leant on her hoe and she began to laugh.

The nearer it came the louder she laughed. She slapped her skinny sides and the tears streamed down her face, which was all crisscross-cobwebbed with lines.

The baby stopped. "What are you laughing at?" it growled, resting its great bulky belly on her gate.

The gate buckled and smashed under the weight of it. Mother Bunch laughed even louder. She pointed at the baby, speechless with glee.

"*What are you laughing at?*" howled the baby, stepping into the garden on its wobbly legs.

Mother Bunch danced in and out of the cabbage patch, round and round the baby. She prodded at it with her hoe. The baby shook with rage. It bent down and tore up a fistful of cabbages. It stuffed the cabbages into its mouth.

"WHAHHAYOUMPHLAUGHMPHINGPHSPLAT?" roared the baby, its mouth full of cabbage.

"You!" shrieked Mother Bunch.

"Me?" said the wooden baby.

"Yes, you, you great big thumping lumpish horror," said Mother Bunch, giving it another prod with the hoe. "Leave my cabbages alone!"

The baby spat out a half-eaten cabbage. "What did you call me?" it demanded furiously.

"A monster," said Mother Bunch.

The baby rolled its eyes. "Right," it said.

"Right what?" said Mother Bunch. "Right what, you silly bushel?"

The baby's face turned purple with fury. Its enormous stomach heaved. In a very quiet and sinister voice it began to sing its song:

> "*I've eaten, I've gobbled:*
> *Some turnip porridge,*
> *One pail of milk,*
> *One loaf of bread,*
> *A tablecloth,*
> *My mummy, my daddy,*
> *A girl with a bicycle,*
> *A farmer with his hay,*

A pigman with his pigs,
A shepherd with his sheep,
Cabbages, cabbages —
And I'm going to eat you too!"

"That," said Mother Bunch, "is what you think." And quick as could be, before the wooden baby had time to jump on her and gobble her up, she pushed her hoe in its belly and cut it open right across.

The wooden baby rolled over on the cabbage patch.

It was dead.

And then, what a sight there was! Because out of the hole Mother Bunch had cut with her hoe in the wooden baby jumped the sheep dog, Mungo. And after Mungo came the shepherd. And after the shepherd the lambs came leaping. Mungo barked. He rounded up all the sheep, and the shepherd whistled, and they all set off for home.

There was a little pause. And then out of the hole Mother Bunch had cut with her hoe in the wooden baby came the pigs, grunting and squealing, followed by the pigman, wiping his hands on his trousers as though he had been somewhere dirty. They set off home after the shepherd.

And then came the horse and cart, and the farmer with his whip, and the little girl with her

brand-new bicycle. And they set off for home after the pigman.

And then, last of all, out jumped the woodcutter and his wife. They were so pleased to be free and alive again that they did a dance for joy, in and out of the cabbages. Mother Bunch shook her head.

"Go home, you silly couple, and be content with what you have," she said.

Mog curtsied. Krog bowed.

"We will! We will!" they cried together. "Oh thank you, Mother Bunch! Thank you very much for saving us from the terrible wooden baby!"

"Rubbish," said Mother Bunch. "I saved you from yourselves."

Krog scratched his head. "I don't understand what you mean," he said slowly.

"Of course you don't," snapped Mother Bunch, "because you haven't got any trousers on!"

Krog looked down. It was true. The wooden baby had not eaten his moleskin trousers and they were still at home. He set off at top speed, his white legs twinkling in the evening sun. And Mog followed after, singing hymns and stopping now and again to think what Mother Bunch could have meant by saying that she had saved them from themselves. But after a while she just sang hymns.

Hung-wu And The Witch's Daughter

In China long ago there lived an old man who
had three sons whose names were Chang, Tung,
and Hung-wu. Chang was tall and Tung was
strong, but Hung-wu was neither tall nor strong
and his father did not think a lot of him. They all
lived in a yellow house in the mountains. Every
day the old man went out to look for sticks to
burn on their fire.

One morning he met a widow in a white dress. She was sitting on a square stone playing chess with a blackbird. The old man liked chess, so he stopped to watch. The blackbird won every time. At last it flew away. The widow looked up.

"Would you like a game?" she asked.

"I would," said the old man.

"Then sit down," said the widow. "But what stakes shall we play for?"

The old man pointed to his bundle of sticks. "We could play for that."

The widow shook her head. "No," she said. "We can't play for sticks because I don't have any sticks. What else have you got?"

"Nothing," said the old man. "I am poor, you see."

"Don't you have any children?" demanded the widow.

"Well, yes," said the old man in surprise. "I have three sons."

The widow clapped her skinny hands. "Just right," she cackled. "I have three daughters. Let us play. If you win, I will send my daughters as brides for your sons. But if I win, you must send me your sons to marry my daughters."

The old man did not much like this idea. But he thought to himself: If she could not beat a blackbird then I am bound to win, for I am certainly a better player than any bird. So he nodded his head and sat down on the square stone.

They played three games and the widow won each game. It was dusk when they finished. The widow stood up and pointed to a dark valley. "That is where I live," she said. "Tomorrow you must send me your eldest son. Three days later, the second son. And three days after that day, the youngest son." Then she gathered all the chessmen in her apron and went off.

The old man returned home. He told his sons what had happened. Chang and Tung were pleased, for they wanted to be married. But Hung-wu was scared when he heard the story, and gnawed at his pigtail.

The next day the old man sent Chang to the widow's house in the dark valley. Three days later, he sent Tung. And three days after that day, he sent Hung-wu.

Hung-wu had not gone far when he met a philosopher wearing a green hat, who asked him where he was going.

"I am going to the house of the widow in the valley," Hung-wu said.

"What for?" asked the philosopher.

"To marry her youngest daughter," said Hung-wu. "My two older brothers are there already. They have married her other daughters."

The philosopher took off his hat and shook the snow from it. "Unfortunately for you," he said, "that widow is a witch. She doesn't have three daughters. She lives in the valley in a big black house, and she has only one daughter. The girl is certainly beautiful, but her mother uses her to trick men to the house and when they come — she kills them! Your brothers are dead. Your eldest brother was eaten by the lion that waits by the outer door. Your second brother was eaten by the tiger that waits by the inner door."

"Oh dear," cried Hung-wu. "What shall I do?"

"Well," said the philosopher, "you were lucky to meet me." He took an iron pearl from his pocket. "Throw this to the lion by the outer door," he said. Then he took an iron rod from his boot. "Give this to the tiger by the inner door," he said. He pointed to a cherry tree that was growing by the stream. "Cut a branch from that tree," he said, "and when you reach the third door, push the door open with it, and you will go in safely enough."

Hung-wu took the pearl and the rod, thanked the philosopher, then went and cut a branch from the cherry tree that grew by the stream. He hurried on down into the dark valley.

Soon he came to a big black house. At the outer door was a lion. He threw the iron pearl to the lion, and the lion began to play with it. Hung-wu went on. At the second door was a tiger. He threw the iron rod to the tiger, and the tiger began to play with it. Hung-wu went on.

The third door was closed tight. He gave it a push with his cherry branch, and

CRASH!

a slab of iron weighing about a thousand pounds fell down as the door opened. The cherry branch was smashed to pulp. If Hung-wu had opened the door with his hand he would have been crushed to death.

The witch was sitting in her room sewing a shroud when she heard the iron slab fall. She smiled at the little blob of blood on her fingertip where the noise had made her prick herself. But she did not smile when Hung-wu came in. She wondered how he had escaped the lion, the tiger, and the iron. However, she pretended to be pleased to see him.

"You've come just in time," she purred. "I have a jar of seeds that I want sown in the field before it rains."

"What about the wedding?" said Hung-wu.

"When you come back, we will have the wedding," the witch replied.

Hung-wu looked out of the window. The sky was full of fat black rain clouds. He took the jar of seeds and went out into the field. But when he got there he found the ground was so thick with weeds that he could not get the seeds in. "How can I sow this field without a hoe or a plough?" he asked himself. He tried to pull up a few weeds, but being neither tall nor strong he soon grew tired, and lying down on the ground he fell asleep.

The wind rose and blew the rain clouds away. The sun shone on Hung-wu. He dreamt of weedings and weddings. When he woke it was evening and the field was full of pigs. The pigs had grubbed about and pulled up all the weeds. Hung-wu was pleased. He thanked the pigs, drove them away, and sowed the seeds. Then he went back to the witch.

"Have you finished the sowing?" she said.

"I have," said Hung-wu.

The witch pulled a thread angrily from the shroud. "Stupid boy," she said. "You didn't look at the sky, did you? All the clouds are gone, the moon is shining bright, no rain will fall, and the seeds won't grow. You will have to go and collect them all again, and not one must be missing."

"What about the wedding?" said Hung-wu.

"When you come back, we will have the wedding."

Hung-wu took the jar and went out into the field to search for the seeds. He looked hard. Soon his fingers were bleeding and his back ached with bending. But he had only found six seeds. He sat down to rest and stared at the moon. "O moon," he said, "I am Hung-wu. I am neither tall nor strong, yet the witch wants me to find all the seeds she made me plant in this rough field. What shall I do?"

The moon did not answer. But when Hung-wu looked about him he saw a strange sight. Hundreds and thousands of red ants were swarming

across the field. Each ant carried a seed. The ants dropped the seeds into the jar, and in no time at all it was full again and spilling with them. Hung-wu thanked the ants and went back to the witch.

"Have you got the seeds?" she demanded.

"Yes," said Hung-wu.

"Every one?" said the witch.

"Every one," said Hung-wu.

He showed her the jar.

The witch blinked and sniffed. "Hmm," she said. "Well, it's far too late at night to have the wedding now. I'm going to sleep."

She shut her eyes, and went.

Next morning the witch said, "Listen, clever one. I am going to hide. If you can find me, we will have the wedding."

Hung-wu rubbed his eyes with his little black pigtail. She had disappeared in a puff of blossom-scented smoke.

Hung-wu searched everywhere for the witch, but he could not find where she was hiding. He did not know what to do, so he sat down and gnawed his pigtail. Then he heard a voice saying, "My mother has hidden in the garden. She has turned herself into a peach on the peach tree. You will recognise the peach because it is half red and half green. The green part is her back, the red part is her cheek. Bite her in the cheek and she will be a woman again."

Hung-wu looked round. He saw at the window a girl in a gown the colour of the sea. Her eyes were like blue jade. Her cheeks reminded him of half-opened lotus flowers. He knew that she must be the witch's daughter. The girl smiled. Hung-wu blushed and ran out into the garden.

The peach tree was against the wall. Hanging on it was one peach, half-green, half-red, just as the witch's daughter had described. Hung-wu snatched it from the tree and bit the red side. The peach melted in his hand. It was gone. Standing in front of him was the witch, with a stream of blood running down her cheek.

"Little one, little one, did you try to kill me?" she screamed.

"Not at all," said Hung-wu. "I was hungry and you — I mean the peach you were — looked quite nice to eat. How could I know you were hiding as fruit?" He grinned. "What about the wedding?" he asked.

The witch glared, mopping her cheek. "When my daughter is married," she said, "she will want a special bed to sleep in. Go to the palace of the Dragon King and fetch me a bed of white jade. When you have done that, we will have the wedding."

Hung-wu's face went white as flour and his knees knocked together loudly when he heard this. The Dragon King lived in Oyster Palace at the bottom of the ocean. No one ever went there. The sea was too deep. Also it had sharks in it. This time the witch seemed to have set him an impossible task.

However, while Hung-wu was standing scratching his head unhappily under the peach tree the witch's daughter appeared from the house. She carried a golden fork in her hand.

"I heard my mother say that you must bring her a bed of white jade from Oyster Palace, where the Dragon King lives," she said.

Hung-wu nodded. The witch's daughter was so beautiful he could not speak when he looked at her.

"Just take this golden fork," said the witch's daughter. "If you draw a line on the sea with it, a road will form and you will be able to go anywhere you want."

Hung-wu, his tongue still in a knot, smiled his thanks and took the fork. He went down to the shore. When he got there he drew a line on the water. The waves rolled back on either side of the line and there in front of him was a salty road leading straight to the palace of the Dragon King. Hung-wu marched down it, his pigtail swinging from side to side.

When he reached Oyster Palace he did not waste time. He saw the Dragon King and told him what he wanted, and why.

"A bed of white jade?" repeated the Dragon King, downing a jellyfish cocktail in one go. "Just look in the store room, my dear boy. There are plenty of white jade beds in there. I can't abide 'em, myself. Give me bad dreams. Choose any one you like, dear boy, and have it with my best wishes. Fancy a jellyfish?"

Hung-wu was pleased. He thanked the Dragon King, managed to avoid a jellyfish, and chose a bed. Then, carrying the bed on his head, he went back along the road which he had carved in the water with the golden fork.

When the witch saw the white jade bed her eyes bristled like buttons. "Clever clever little one," she purred. "Clever clever clever little pigtail!" And she seized Hung-wu's pigtail in her skinny hands and twisted it hard, all the time smiling as though this was a friendly thing to do.

"What about the wedding?" demanded Hung-wu.

"Ah, ah, the wedding, the wedding," chanted the witch, making out that she had forgotten about it. "Listen, pigtail. In the west, on the mountain of the Monkey King, there is a big drum. We will need it for the celebrations. Go to the mountain of the Monkey King and fetch me that big drum. When you have done that, we will have the wedding."

Hung-wu shivered all the way down to his toe-nails. He had heard that the Monkey King was fierce and wild. He lived on Desolation Mountain. Still, Hung-wu knew that he would have to go.

Just as he was leaving the house, the witch's daughter appeared again. "What task has my mother set you now?" she asked.

Fear helped Hung-wu speak to her. "I have to go and fetch the big drum from Desolation Mountain, the home of the Monkey King," he explained.

The witch's daughter sat down and thought for a moment. First she rested her head on her right hand, then on her left. Then she said, "I can tell you that the Monkey King has gone on a long journey to the Western Heaven and has not yet returned to Desolation Mountain. Now, below the mountain there is a lake of mud. Whenever the Monkey King comes home he jumps into that lake and rolls around. If you jump into it and roll around like the Monkey King, the little monkeys will think you are their master and will do anything you say. Here is a needle, a packet of lime, and a bottle of oil. Take these things with you. If you are in any danger, throw them over your shoulder — first the needle, then the lime, lastly the oil."

Hung-wu thanked the witch's daughter for her help. When he came to the lake of mud below Desolation Mountain he held his nose between his right thumb and forefinger and jumped into it —

PLOP!

Then he rolled about in the sucky mud until his whole body was caked in it. Only his eyes showed, so that he could see where he was going. Then he hurried up the mountain.

The little monkeys swung down from the trees when they saw him coming. "Master!" they cried. "You've come home early!"

"Yes," growled Hung-wu in the deepest voice he could manage. "I came to see how you behave yourselves while I am away on monkey business."

The little monkeys carried him up the mountain on a purple throne with poles at each end. When they reached the top they set the throne down. Hung-wu clapped his hands. "Your master has come a long way and is very hungry," he shouted. "Go and get me peaches from the peach orchard and be quick about it!"

Off ran the little monkeys, squealing, to do his bidding.

When the last one was safely out of sight Hung-wu slid from the throne and ran to a silver pavilion that stood nearby. Inside the silver pavilion hung the big drum. He cut the strings that held it, balanced it on his shoulder, and set off as fast as he could down the mountainside. He had not gone far when he heard the monkeys coming after him. One of them had seen him steal the drum. "Stop!" they shouted. "Trickster! Thief! You pretended to be our master. Then you stole our big drum. You just wait till we catch you!"

Hung-wu took the needle from his muddy pocket. He threw it behind him. As soon as it hit the ground there was a needle mountain between him and the angry monkeys. The monkeys tore their skin and scratched their eyes on it, but it did not stop them. They howled and screamed as they came over the needle mountain.

Hung-wu took the packet of lime the witch's daughter had given him and threw it over his shoulder. As soon as that hit the ground there was a mountain of lime between him and the monkeys. With their torn skin and blind eyes some of the monkeys got stuck in the lime and died. But the rest still chased him, angrier than ever.

Hung-wu took the bottle of oil from his pocket. He threw it behind him. The bottle burst, and the oil came pouring out. Immediately there was a slippery mountain between him and the monkeys. When the monkeys tried to climb up the slippery mountain, they slipped straight down again, and when they climbed up again, they slipped straight down again. . . . So Hung-wu escaped, washed all the mud off in a stream, and returned to the witch before the sun had set.

"Surely it is time for the wedding now?" Hung-wu said to the witch, when he had given her the big drum of the Monkey King.

The witch pointed with her finger to the sun. "It's early yet," she whined. "My daughter will need a net to keep the mosquitoes from her bed of white jade. Just go into the garden and cut down two bamboo sticks. When you come back, we will have the wedding."

Hung-wu thought to himself: Two bamboo sticks? That sounds too easy to be true.

He went to the witch's daughter. He did not feel so frightened of her being beautiful now, so he told her what her mother had asked him to do and asked her what was terrible about the garden.

"What is terrible about the garden," said the witch's daughter, "is the gardener. His name is Nung-kua-ma and he has a body like a bull, a head like a tiger, and sharp teeth and claws. He likes to tear off people's skins and eat their fingers."

Hung-wu bit his pigtail. His eyes rolled. "What can I do against such a monster?" he stammered.

The witch's daughter went to a long lacquered chest and took out a coat of coconut, ten small reeds, and a two-edged hachet. She hung the coat on Hung-wu's shoulders, fitted the bamboo reeds on his fingers, and gave him the two-edged hatchet to hold. "Be as quick as you can," she said, "and you will come to no harm."

Hung-wu thanked her and went into the garden. He found the bamboo and cut down two sticks with his hatchet. Just at that moment the gardener came out of the thicket. "AAAAAAAA AAAAAAAAAAAAAAAAAAAAAA," he roared. His claws caught Hung-wu and stripped the skin from his back — only it was not Hung-wu's skin that came off, only the coconut coat. Then Nung-kua-ma the terrible gardener used his sharp teeth to bite off Hung-wu's fingers — only it was not the fingers that he crunched, only the ten small reeds. He stuffed the coat and the reeds into his hairy mouth and began to eat them, stamping his feet as he did so. Hung-wu ran off.

The witch was playing dice with dead men's bones. When she saw that Hung-wu had escaped from Nung-kua-ma and brought the bamboo for the mosquito net, she said, "Clever clever little one, clever clever clever clever little one! Oh how clever you are, little pigtail!"

Hung-wu was wise to her tricks. He skipped out of reach when she made to twist his pigtail. "I have sown seeds and gathered seeds," he said. "I have found you when you hid in the likeness of a peach. I have brought you a bed of white jade from Oyster Palace where the Dragon King lives, and a big drum for celebrations from Desolation Mountain where the Monkey King lives. Also bamboo for a mosquito net to keep your daughter comfortable at night. Surely now it is time for the wedding?"

To his surprise, the witch patted him on the head. "Yes, dear," she said. "It *is* time for the wedding." She pinched his cheek. "But first," she said thoughtfully, "you really must have something to eat. You haven't eaten all day, have you, pigtail? You must be very hungry."

"I am," Hung-wu admitted.

"In the black pot in the kitchen you will find some noodles," said the witch. "Eat them first. When you come back, we will have the wedding."

Hung-wu hurried to the kitchen. He was so hungry. He took the lid off the black pot. There were lovely white noodles inside. He grabbed a handful and stuffed them into his mouth. Soon he felt a terrible pain. He rolled on the floor and kicked his legs in agony.

The kitchen door opened. It was the witch's daughter. "What is the matter?" she cried.

Gasping, Hung-wu told her.

"Quick!" she said. "Take off your shoes and hang upside-down on that beam there!"

"But why —?"

"Don't argue!"

Hung-wu shook off his shoes and hung from the beam upside-down with his knees bent over it and his pigtail trailing the floor. The witch's daughter snatched a shoe in either hand and began beating him with them. Before long, a snake fell out of Hung-wu's mouth. And then another. And then another. Soon there were ten small white snakes wriggling and writhing on the floor. The witch's daughter went on beating Hung-wu with the shoes until he had coughed up all the snakes.

Then she helped him down. "My mother always wants to harm you," she said. "Those were snakes you ate, not noodles. It is lucky you are not dead. Go straightaway and ask my mother to have the wedding now."

Hung-wu thanked her, and did as she said.

The witch stamped and cursed and tore out handfuls of her own hair, but she could think of no more tasks or excuses, and she had to agree to the wedding taking place the next evening.

The wedding of Hung-wu and the witch's daughter was a magnificent affair. The big drum of the Monkey King was beaten. The bed of white jade from the palace of the Dragon King stood ready for them in a huge hall, with a mosquito net made from bamboo hanging over it. But when Hung-wu and his bride approached the bed they found a golden river flowing down the middle of it.

"This is another magic of my mother's," said the witch's daughter.

She searched everywhere for the source of the spell. At last, in a cupboard, she found a jug of tea with a bit of wood floating in it. She took out the wood, emptied the tea on the floor, and the river vanished at once.

"We must run away," she whispered to her husband. "If we stay here, my mother will cer-certainly try to kill us."

She snatched up a blue umbrella and a chicken, gave them both to her husband to carry, and they fled away in the middle of the night.

The moon shone bright yellow on the Chinese

mountains. They had not gone far when they heard a whirring sound above their heads. The witch's daughter opened the blue umbrella and beckoned Hung-wu to shelter with her beneath it.

"My mother has sent a flying knife after us," she said. "If the knife smells blood, it falls. Throw out the chicken, and the knife will kill it."

Hung-wu did as he was told. The knife flashed down. The chicken squawked. Then it was dead.

They hurried on along the mountain road. But the witch's daughter got a stitch. She had to stop for breath.

"Listen!" she cried.

Hung-wu listened. He could hear the whirring sound high in the air again.

"It's the flying knife," hissed the witch's daughter, as they cowered beneath the blue umbrella. "It's come back! Chicken blood is sweet. Human blood is salty. My mother knows she did not kill us last time. What can we do?"

Hung-wu felt brave because he loved her. "I will step out," he said, "and sacrifice myself."

"No, no," said the witch's daughter. "I must die, because I can come to life again. When I am dead just carry my body home with you and buy a big pail to put it in. In seven times seven days I shall come to life again."

So saying, and before Hung-wu could stop her, she stepped out from beneath the shelter of the blue umbrella. He heard the knife zoom down.

Then its noise ceased. Hung-wu saw his bride lying on the ground. Her eyes were closed. Her face was as pale as pear blossom. The knife was stuck in her heart and blood was pouring out. Hung-wu wiped away his tears with his little black pigtail and carried her body to his home.

It was dawn when he reached his father's house. He told his father all that had happened. The old man wept when he heard how Chang and Tung had been killed by the witch. But Hung-wu bought a big pail, put his bride's body in it, put the lid on, and watched and waited.

After forty-eight days, Hung-wu heard groans and moans coming from the pail, as if someone was in unbearable pain. He thought to himself: If I don't let her out now, but wait another day, she might die again.

So he took the lid off the pail.

The witch's daughter lifted up her head slowly and looked at him. "Why did you uncover me a day too soon?" she said. "Obviously we are not meant for each other after all."

Tears ran down her face. Then her head sank back and her eyes closed. She was dead for ever.